*Also available from Hodder Children's Books
in a two-in-one special edition*

Jackie Won a Pony
Jackie and the Pony Trekkers

A Hodder Children's Books two-in-one
special edition

Jackie and the Pony Camp Summer
Jackie and the Pony-Boys

Jackie and the Pony Camp Summer

Judith M. Berrisford

Hodder
Children's
Books

a division of Hodder Headline plc

For Ian McNeillie, Chris Baker, Stuart Dick, Raymond and
Derek Jones

Special two-in-one edition published 1996
by Hodder Children's Books
ISBN 0 340 68735 5

10 9 8 7 6 5 4 3 2 1

Jackie and the Pony Camp Summer
Copyright © 1968 Judith M. Berrisford
First published in Great Britain in 1968 by
Brockhampton Press Ltd

A Catalogue record for this book is available from the British Library

Offset by Avon Dataset Ltd, Bidford-on-Avon, Warks
Printed and bound in Great Britain by
Cox & Wyman Ltd, Reading, Berks

Hodder Children's Books
a division of Hodder Headline plc
338 Euston Road
London NW1 3BH

Contents

CHAPTER ONE

NEW PONY FRIENDS

My cousin Babs and I halted our ponies as we reached the crest of the grassy hill. We looked towards a cluster of pink-washed farm buildings. A group of tents in a meadow beyond showed white against the fresh green of the headland which sloped to rocks and a sandy beach.

Sunlight gilded the tidepools, and foamy wavelets lapped against the sea's edge.

We turned our gaze back to the headland and the tents. So this was the Pony Camp where we were going to be helpers for the rest of the summer holidays.

'Where is everybody?' I said, because, at the moment, the camp seemed oddly deserted.

'They're probably all out on a picnic ride,' said Babs, touching Patch with her heels. 'Come on. Let's investigate.'

Soon we were dismounting in the cobbled stable-yard. I looked towards the empty stables.

'Hello!' I called. 'Anyone there?'

Just then a ginger head appeared through the open window of a hayloft, and a boy shouted: 'Shan't be a jiffy,' and immediately disappeared.

Then, strangely, only a few moments later, a ginger-haired boy in a yellow shirt and faded blue jeans strolled round the corner of the stables.

'Hi!' Babs called. 'I'm Babs Spencer, and this is my cousin, Jackie Hope.'

'And I'm Paul Wayne,' replied the boy. Then as we shook hands, we heard footsteps on some wooden stairs, and another ginger-haired boy appeared. I blinked in surprise, thinking that I was seeing double. Both boys were identical from their ginger heads, blue eyes and freckled faces to their yellow shirts and faded jeans.

'Twins,' exclaimed Babs. 'However are we going to tell you two apart?'

'Most people don't,' said the newcomer. 'I'm Pete and he's Paul.' He smiled. 'I like the look of your ponies.'

The twins made a fuss of Misty and Patch

before taking us to the stable near the loose-boxes to unhitch our kit and unsaddle our ponies. We left Misty and Patch pulling at hay nets in the sweet-smelling dimness. Beside them was another pony who, in the gloom, might easily have been mistaken for Patch although, on closer look, I saw that he was really black and white – a piebald – whereas Bab's Patch was skewbald – brown and white.

Pete – or was it Paul? – put his hand on the piebald's withers and fondly straightened his mane.

'This is Magpie,' he said. 'He's in here because he's waiting to have a shoe fixed. The other ponies are out on a ride with the campers. They'll all be back for high tea at six.'

'In the meantime,' said the other twin, 'we'll help you to put up your tent so that you can settle in. Then perhaps you can give us a hand to get a meal ready for the campers.'

We pitched our green ridge tent, put down the groundsheet and pumped up our air mattresses. Then, hanging our jackets from hooks on the tent pole, we rolled up our sleeves and followed the boys to a canvas shelter which was erected over a field kitchen.

While the boys kindled the fire and piled on

sawn-up branches, Babs and I examined the food store. There were big cans of soup, vast tins of baked beans, fruit, jam, and plenty of dehydrated mashed potatoes.

'What's for tea?' Babs asked.

'Sausages and chips – and that means peeling all these,' said Pete, dragging out a carton of potatoes.

Babs and I dipped the potatoes into a bucket of water and peeled while the boys sliced. By the time the campers returned, hot, tired and hungry, the fat was bubbling merrily, and an outsize basket of chips was beginning to brown.

Babs shook the chip basket from time to time, while I prodded the sausages in the large frying pan with a fork.

'Good work!' said an approving voice, and we looked up to see an auburn-haired young woman, of about twenty-one or so, the twins' sister, Sheila. She introduced us to the campers – five girls and four boys, aged from about eleven to sixteen.

After tea and washing up, in which the campers helped, Sheila and Pete took us to meet the rest of the ponies, while Paul held Magpie for the blacksmith who had just arrived.

'We've only got ten ponies at the moment,'

Sheila explained, leading the way to a field where all the ponies were turned out to graze.

'Plus Misty and Patch,' offered Babs. 'You can borrow them if you're short. How many campers are there going to be?'

'Well, let me see,' said Sheila. 'Eight are going home tomorrow, and another ten are arriving.'

'So you're really fully booked,' said Babs.

'Oh, no,' said Sheila. 'We can always put up more tents and get more ponies if other people want to come. The more the merrier.'

I looked across the paddock, beyond a drystone wall, where the Waynes' ponies were grazing.

They were mostly about fourteen hands high – two browns; a dun with the wild-horse black line down his back and with a long black tail; two roans – one strawberry and one blue; a chestnut with a bright mane and tail; a black; one bay with dark points, and one bay with a light mane and tail.

'Hey, Daydream.' Sheila gave a soft whistle, and the bay with dark points came trotting up to her. 'We usually keep her up because she's a show-jumper,' she told us. 'But she's out in the field today with the others for a change.'

'Sheila!' shouted one of the campers from the farmhouse doorway. 'Trunk call. A brother and sister from Epping want to book up for the week after next.'

She smiled at Babs and me. 'Business is getting brisk. You're bringing us luck. Something tells me we'll make a success of this Pony Camp.'

'Cross your fingers for luck!' I said quickly, and thought: you wouldn't have said that, Sheila, if you'd known what a pair of jinxes Babs and I are supposed to be.

CHAPTER TWO

THE DIFFICULT TWIN

I was still admiring the bay pony, who stood near me hoping for sugar, while Sheila hurried to answer the telephone.

'Daydream's a beauty,' I said to Pete, running my hand down her neck and patting her firm withers, while I admired her firm bone and springy hocks. 'I'd love to try her.'

'Well then, jump up,' said Pete. 'You won't need a saddle. She's perfectly quiet.'

I climbed on to Daydream's back from the wall and she moved off at once with an easy gait.

'Come on, girl.'

I touched her with my heels and she broke into a smooth trot. Then we cantered. Round the paddock she went, answering to my legs and to the touch of my hands on her neck.

'She's like a mind-reader,' I said, halting her

in front of Pete and Babs. 'She seems to know exactly what one wants her to do without any need for a bridle.'

'Yes, she's wonderful, isn't she?' Pete agreed, rubbing the bay pony affectionately between the eyes. 'Would you like to try her over a jump?'

'Could I?'

'I don't see why not,' said Pete. 'You managed her jolly well just now, and she's a willing jumper.'

'Lucky you,' Babs said to me enviously, as Pete went to the stables and came back a few moments later carrying a pole and two light-weight trestles which he fixed up to make a low cavaletti.

'There you are,' he said, stepping back. 'Instant obstacles. Try her over that, Jackie.'

Daydream gave an excited toss of the head when I rode her towards the cavaletti. It was obvious that she loved jumping. I touched her with my heels, and she broke into a canter. Steadily, with perfect timing, she approached the jump. She took off effortlessly and sailed over. She jumped like a dream, I thought. No wonder she was called Daydream.

I rode her round the field. Then I put her at the jump once more. Again she gave that pleased toss of the head. Neck extended, she approached the jump, tucked her forefeet well up, took off and was over.

'Well done,' called Babs, and Pete turned round the trestles to make the jump higher.

'Try that,' he urged.

As I approached the jump a whinny came from the stables, and there was a thud of hooves. I turned to see my pony, Misty, cantering towards the paddock.

'Look out,' Babs warned. 'Misty's jealous.'

I groaned. Misty must have heard us making a fuss of Daydream, and now, not wanting to be left out of anything, she was coming to see what was happening.

'Go back, Misty,' I called, halting Daydream and waving my pony away from the paddock. Babs scrambled over the wall and ran to catch her. Misty swung out of Bab's reach and jumped into the field.

Mischief in her eyes, my pony was coming straight for me and Daydream.

'Oh Misty, you bad pony,' I sighed, sliding off Daydream and running to catch Misty who brushed past me, knocking me sideways. Eyes rolling, she went up to Daydream, darted her neck forward and gave the bay a nip on the withers. Daydream backed, kicked and caught one of the other ponies. Pete ran to catch her, and the other ponies, startled, jostled together in a foot-stamping huddle at the far end.

'What's happening?' exclaimed a boy's voice, and we turned to see Paul staring at the milling group of ponies, while he hitched Magpie to the gate. 'For goodness' sake!' he groaned, running into the field. 'Grab that grey pony before she does any more damage. Pinky looks as if he's been lamed, and if any of the others get kicked they'll be out of action for a week, just when we need every pony for the campers.'

'Don't flap, Paul,' said his twin over his shoulder as he helped Babs and me to corner Misty. I grabbed Misty, and Pete turned to face Paul. 'Pinky isn't really lame,' he declared, running gentle hands down the strawberry roan's off-hind. 'It was only a brush.'

'All the same, it might have been serious,' Paul pointed out. 'Anyway, Pete, I think you ought to have known better than to let a strange girl ride Daydream bareback, and try to jump her. I thought we'd decided to put all the jumps away.' He turned to Babs and me. 'How did your pony get out of the stable? You can't have tied her up properly or shut the door.'

I felt guilty. I suppose we'd been so thrilled at arriving at the camp and seeing everybody that we'd given Misty a hay net and left her to it It was quite possible that we'd been too excited to tie her up securely or to shut the door, as Paul said.

'I'm sorry, Paul,' I said soberly. 'I suppose we have been careless.'

'And because of that,' Paul replied, 'a pony's been kicked. Well, you've been lucky. It might have been serious.' He moved across to Misty. 'This pony isn't to be trusted with the others yet awhile.' He turned to me. 'Is she always so vicious?'

'Misty hasn't an ounce of vice in her,' Babs said, rushing to my pony's defence. 'She's a sweet, good-tempered pony.'

'Good-tempered ponies don't bite,' Paul said. 'She'll have to be kept apart from the others until we see how she's going to settle down.'

We turned to Pete. What did he think? Would he back us up?

'Better do as Paul says, Jackie,' he said quietly.

Feeling deflated, Babs and I took Misty back to join Patch in the stables, while Paul walked towards the farmhouse followed by Pete.

'That's done it,' Babs said ruefully. 'We're in disgrace already. I suppose it was our fault, but, oh dear, I'll never understand why Paul got so cross when Pete didn't make any fuss at all.'

'I expect we deserve it,' I said sadly. 'We usually do.' I turned to my pony. 'Oh, Misty,' I scolded. 'You have been a bad pony letting us down like that just when Babs and I were trying to make a good impression.'

Misty rubbed her nose against my sleeve as if to tell me that she was sorry. With a sigh, I put her back into the stable. As she pulled at her hay, Babs and I walked back towards the house, still feeling downhearted.

'Not to worry!' Sheila greeted us. 'Mishaps will happen. I saw it all through the window.' She looked at dark clouds which were gathering in the evening sky. 'We're all going to the big barn for a pony quiz until the storm's over. You know a lot about ponies. So here's your chance to shine. Come on – cheer up.'

CHAPTER THREE

OTHER PEOPLE'S PONIES

Miracle of miracles! I won the pony quiz, and Babs came second. Sheila presented us with a pony book each as prizes, and we hoped that we were in favour again as one of the twins patted us on our backs in congratulation.

'Thanks, Paul,' I said.

'I'm Pete,' he told me with a friendly smile, and I looked across the barn with a sinking heart, to see that Paul's back was turned on us as he looked out of the window. Well, we'd just have to try harder and hope to earn his approval. It did seem strange that Pete was so kind and friendly, while Paul had quickly become grumpy and hostile as if he'd taken a dislike to me and Babs.

Just then Sheila began to play a jangly piano, and everyone started a sing-song.

An hour later, hoarse but happy, we joined

the other campers in a dash over the wet grass to our tents. We were asleep almost as soon as our heads touched the air pillows.

Next morning we were awakened by the sound of a hunting horn just outside our tent.

'Breakfast's ready,' Pete called. 'Come and get it.'

'Where have you two been?' demanded Paul, as Babs and I appeared after hurriedly scrambling into our clothes. 'Sheila could have done with your help in getting the breakfast. It's up early in the morning here, you know.'

'Sorry,' I said meekly. 'We'll be sure to be in time to help tomorrow.'

Sheila handed everyone large plates full of bacon, tomato, sausages and fried bread. 'We may only have time for a scratch lunch,' she told Babs and me. 'So eat plenty now. Then perhaps you'll lend a hand cleaning up the house.'

We were flipping round with dusters and mop when a telephone bell rang. Pete ran to answer it. 'Just a minute,' he said, in reply to an excited young voice over the line. 'I'll have to ask my sister.'

Putting his hand over the mouthpiece he called through the open window to Sheila who was in the yard checking Magpie's shoes. 'It's those three boys from Milltown. They're not going on their school trip to Paris after all. So they want to know if they can come here instead. Can they come today?'

Sheila thought for a moment, and then quickly made up her mind.

'Yes, we'll fit them in somehow,' she decided, and as Pete noted down the time that the boys would need picking up from the station with their kit, she said to us: 'Never turn customers away. That's rule number one for a successful business.'

'And rule number two,' said Paul, with a trace of grumpiness, 'is make sure that there is a pony for every camper before you accept more bookings.'

'I've thought of that,' Sheila said, undaunted. 'I've fixed up to borrow extra mounts from the Rivermouth Stables. We need someone to ride over to fetch them.' She turned to me. 'Would you like to go with Pete?'

I agreed readily.

'Well, my advice is: if you let Jackie go, don't let her take Misty,' advised Paul. 'That mare would probably bite the other ponies.'

I was about to stick up for Misty. Then I thought: what's the use? After all, Misty had been jealous of Daydream, and had definitely given her a nip, so Paul had a point there.

'Take my pony,' Babs offered.

As I saddled Patch, I had some misgivings. Somehow I felt nervous every time I thought of Paul, and that made me do things wrong. If only Paul could be identical with Pete in character, as well as in looks. Pete was so happy-go-lucky, and he obviously liked Babs and me.

I trotted Patch into the lane, humming to myself and trying to shake off my thoughts about the difficult twin. Pete recognized the tune and whistled in harmony as he jogged ahead of me on Daydream.

I rode close to the verge, keeping Patch well under control. Passing traffic came near, often fast, and I knew the risk of being absent-minded or scatter-brained at such times.

Coming back along the road would be the test, with our own two ponies and three strange ones as well. If anything went wrong, Paul would be sure to say: 'I told you so.'

'We're nearly there,' Pete called over his shoulder, cutting into my forebodings. 'First turning on the left.'

The Rivermouth Stables were grander than I had imagined. Purpose-built loose boxes lined an orderly stable-yard. Neat signs on the doors proclaimed TACK ROOM AND OFFICE.

Dismounting and tying Patch and Daydream to a hitching bar, Pete and I went to the door marked OFFICE, and knocked.

'Come in,' called a voice, and we walked in to find a youth of about nineteen blinking at us through heavy, horn-rimmed spectacles.

'Yes?' he queried, eyebrows raised.

'We've come for the ponies,' said Pete.

'Oh, have you?' the youth said, in surprise. 'I rather expected Miss Wayne to come in person. However – ' He took off his spectacles and tapped them on some papers in a self-important way '– perhaps you'd better read through this.'

He pushed forward a typewritten document. I peered over Pete's shoulder to read:

I hereby take delivery of the three under-mentioned ponies

Pixie – brown with white stockings on near-hind, and white hairs on withers, fourteen h.h.

Strawberry – roan with white blaze and black mane. Six years old, thirteen-three h.h.

Bobbin – bay with black points, fourteen-two h.h.

I certify that they were sound and in good condition on receipt; and that I will be fully responsible for returning them in the same condition on or before the fifth of next September, or whenever required to do so by their owner – H. Stanley Morrison, Rivermouth Stables, Ringbury.

Signed.................

date

'Well, that's easy,' I said. 'Pete and I will sign it, and then we can take the ponies.'

'But you're both minors,' the youth pointed out, 'and this is a legally binding document and must be signed by someone over twenty-one. Those three ponies are worth a great deal of money.' He waved his spectacles at us. 'I'm sure you'll appreciate that my father has to have some safeguard.'

Pete looked crestfallen. 'I suppose so,' he said. 'But more campers are arriving today along with three boys who weren't expected until later. They'll all want to ride this afternoon. We need the ponies now.'

'I've got it!' I said. 'Pete is Sheila's brother, and the Pony Camp is a joint enterprise run by the Wayne family. Let Pete sign and put on behalf of Sheila Wayne.'

The youth looked doubtful. 'It doesn't seem quite right to me. We've got to have a grown-up signature as well. Oh, very well.' He handed Pete a ball-point pen. 'Both of you sign one of these carbons and then I'll give you the top copy to take back to the camp. Please get Sheila to sign it, and see that it's posted back to us this afternoon. Okay?'

Pete and I followed the youth across the stable-yard to a range of looseboxes where the three ponies were waiting already saddled and bridled, their stirrup irons run up to the top of their leathers.

'Mount your own ponies,' suggested the youth, 'and then I'll hand you the reins of these when you're ready.'

With Pete leading Pixie and Strawberry, and me leading Bobbin, on our near sides, we walked our mounts through the gate and on to the road.

'What a lot of red tape!' said Pete, breaking into a trot. 'I thought we were never going to get the ponies.'

'And what a stuffy young man,' I echoed feelingly. 'He sounded more like eighty instead of eighteen.'

'He's got ambitions to be a lawyer,' said Pete, 'so that probably accounts for it. He's never been very horsy, either. All the same, I suppose one can't blame him for being fussy. These are valuable horses. Perhaps we'd better not take them on the main road. We can get back to camp via the country lanes, but it's two miles longer.'

'Better be slow than sorry,' I said, as we turned down a quiet road.

Strawberry and Pixie seemed to go quietly enough beside Daydream, though Bobbin was quite jumpy. He kept twitching a muscle on his flank, and giving a dancing step. He didn't really seem as calm as he should have done for a staid pony, guaranteed safe for beginners. However, I was not very worried. I felt that I could control him well enough from Patch's back.

Suddenly Bobbin shied at a paper bag in the hedge and cannoned into us, squashing my leg against Patch's side, and banging my knee on the saddle.

'Hey, look out,' I warned Bobbin. 'Ah well, I suppose I'd better ride you, and lead Patch.' I reined up and called: 'Wait a minute, Pete.'

I slid down from Patch's back and sorted out the reins before mounting Bobbin. Just then a motor scooter careered round the bend and raced noisily past.

Bobbin snorted and shied, dragging his reins from my fingers. He wheeled, plunged across the verge and jumped the hedge. There was a frightened squeal, and then he disappeared from view.

With a sick feeling in my tummy I scrambled up the hedge bank and looked over. There, in a deep hidden ditch, lay the pony, quite still.

Leading the other three ponies, Pete hurried to the bank.

'He isn't moving,' he reported. 'Here, hold these.'

He passed me the ponies' reins and clambered over the hedge as Strawberry, one of the other Rivermouth ponies, lifted her head and whinnied, sensing that something was wrong with her stable-mate.

The whinny seemed to bring Bobbin back to life. His sides heaved as he took a deep breath. Then he threshed his hooves, trying to roll over to get up, but his efforts seemed to make him slip farther into the muddy ditch. He slid on to his back and, still struggling, wedged himself tighter.

Pete scrambled down the bank. He stood ankle-deep in mud beside the threshing pony.

'Steady, Bobbin.' He grasped the pony's bridle and heaved to no avail. Bobbin still lay struggling. 'He'll burst his guts if we don't get him out soon.' Pete was getting desperate. 'What we need is a rope and a tractor. Tie the other ponies up, Jackie, and take Patch for help.'

I put a foot into Patch's stirrup ready to mount to ride to the nearest farm. Just then I heard the peep of a car horn, and an old taxi came round the bend with luggage strapped and roped to its roof-rack. I took my foot out of the stirrup and, pulling Patch behind me, ran across the verge and into the middle of the road, holding up my hand to flag the taxi to a halt.

The plump taxi-driver leaned anxiously out of the window. 'Anything wrong, love?'

'Plenty,' I said feelingly, and turned to see several boys and girls in the back. The girls were wearing jodhpurs. 'Pony people – thank heavens!' I gasped. 'I expect you're on the way to the Pony Camp. I'm a helper there. So please come to the rescue.'

'What's wrong?' asked one boy.

'It's a pony. He's stuck in a ditch on the other side of the hedge,' I explained. 'He's on his back, and if we don't get him out quickly he may rupture himself and have to be shot. We need ropes.'

'Quick!' Pete's desperate voice floated over the hedge. 'Hurry! I can't keep him still.'

CHAPTER FOUR

TRYING TO HELP

'Coming, sonny!' The fat taxi-driver lumbered
breathlessly into the field while we tugged at
the knots of the rope holding the luggage.

By now all the others were helping. We
disentangled the ropes and straps, and buckled
and knotted them in one strong length. My
fingers fumbled as I slid the last buckle home.
Then, carrying our improvised rope between
us, we hurried into the field.

In the ditch, Pete and the taxi-driver were
standing one on either side of Bobbin, encouraging him to keep still so that he would not
strain himself.

We passed the 'rope' to Pete who fastened
it to the front of Bobbin's running martingale
which, luckily, was not broken. Then, leaving
the taxi driver in the ditch to help the pony,
the rest of us took up our position on the

bank, holding the rope like a tug-of-war team. We pulled, but nothing happened.

'We're just not strong enough,' groaned one of the boys. 'It would take more than us to move that pony and get him back on his feet.'

One of the girls, who was called Wendy, looked round for inspiration, and her eyes caught the roof of the taxi. 'I know!' She scrambled down into the ditch to replace the taxi-driver at Bobbin's side. 'If you can bring the taxi into the field,' she told the plump man, 'we could fasten the rope to that.'

The driver backed his vehicle through the gate and over the grass.

'The bumper won't stand the strain, I reckon,' he grunted. He lowered himself on to the grass and wriggled on his back under the taxi to buckle one end of the rope round the axle-case. Then, puffing his way out with difficulty, he stood up and got into the driving seat to put the taxi into gear while we all stood ready to push, shove and hoist Bobbin to his feet.

The taxi's wheels spun before they gained a hold in the soft ground. The rope strained and the leather creaked. With a squelch of mud, Bobbin was pulled first to his knees, and then, lumberingly, to his feet. He stood trembling before scrambling out of the ditch.

'Hurrah!' panted Wendy, patting the frightened pony. 'I never thought we'd do it.'

Pete plucked handfuls of long grass from the hedge and, using them with his handkerchief, rubbed Bobbin down, while one of the girls removed his saddle.

'He's breaking into a sweat,' said Pete. 'Get some more grass, Jackie, and rub him down on the other side. He'll get a chill if we're not careful.'

Suddenly Bobbin's ears pricked, and he gave a neigh. An answering neigh from the gate made us look round to see a serious-looking man, with a moustache, dismounting from a chestnut horse.

'What's happened to Bobbin?' the man asked in a stern voice.

'Er, hullo, Mr Morrison,' gasped Pete, and we realized that this was Bobbin's owner and the father of the stuffy young man who was so legally minded.

'Nothing to worry about,' I told Mr Morrison in what I meant to be a reassuring voice. 'It's all over and no harm done.'

'The pony was in a proper fix, sir,' the taxi-driver said. 'But these youngsters did the right thing.'

I looked anxiously at Mr Morrison. He didn't

seem reassured by the taxi-driver's words. 'I don't want to make difficulties for you,' he said to Pete, 'but I've got to consider my ponies. They're my stock-in-trade. In fact my livelihood depends on them.' He took off his jacket and put it across Bobbin's loins. 'I can't risk letting you take him to your camp. He'll have to come back to my stables.'

'But, Mr Morrison – ' Pete protested and stopped as Mr Morrison turned away to look at Strawberry and Pixie who were standing by the hedge.

'I can't manage the three of them myself,' Mr Morrison said firmly. 'Perhaps two of you will be good enough to bring the other two ponies along for me.'

Pete stared at Mr Morrison in dismay. 'Please give us another chance and let us keep Strawberry and Pixie,' he begged. 'If you don't, we shall be short of ponies for the camp.'

'I couldn't risk it.' Mr Morrison shook his head. 'Sorry. Now be reasonable and don't let us have any argument about this.'

With heavy hearts, Pete and I mounted our ponies, and led Strawberry and Pixie behind Mr Morrison, back to his stables from which we had collected them an hour earlier. Meanwhile, the campers got back into the taxi which squelched out of the field and started on its way again towards the Pony Camp.

Pony Camp! I thought as its engine faded behind the clip-clop of our ponies' hooves. What kind of a Pony Camp would it be without the three extra ponies which Sheila had been counting on? What would she say when we got back and told our woeful news? Worse still, what would Paul say?

Of course Paul was furious –
I was sitting on my camp-bed, writing to Mummy and Daddy that evening.

And I must admit it's a bind because, with three ponies short, it means that Babs and I will have to lend Misty and Patch to the campers, and we and one of the twins will have to stay behind to do camp chores while the others go off for picnic rides. Sheila was disappointed, but she made the best of it, knowing that things always do go wrong from time to time wherever there are ponies.

But to get back to Pete and Paul. Considering that they're twins and look exactly alike, it's odd now different they are in character. Pete's always friendly and jolly and seems to take life as it comes and enjoys every moment, but Paul's somehow soured. If anything goes wrong he gets cross and always seems to blame it on Babs and me.

Babs wonders whether he's a girl-hater. But I don't know. He doesn't seem to like anybody. He gets a bit short with Pete, too. But Pete and Sheila just seem to accept his bad temper. You'd think they'd just tell him not to be so grumpy. But they never do. Perhaps they've tried, and found it makes him worse.

Meanwhile we're still in the middle of a pony flap – or should I say ponyless flap? Six more campers are due to arrive tomorrow and then we shall be nine ponies short. Sheila's been phoning round to all the other stables and she hasn't been able to get a single pony. The owner of one of the stables was quite nasty to her. It seems she'd heard about the mishap to Mr Morrison's Bobbin, and she wasn't risking anything like that happening to one of her mounts.

Well, more news, probably even more dire, in a few days.

Your loving daughter,
Jackie

35

The other six campers, four girls and two boys, arrived soon after tea next day. Babs and I helped them to put up two tents. Just as we were tightening the guy lines of the girls' tents, and showing them how to roll up the brailings, Pete sounded the hunting horn that the Waynes used to call the campers together.

We gathered round to see Sheila standing in the middle of the field, a sheet of paper in her hand.

'As you know, we're short of ponies,' she told the campers. 'So, until we get some more mounts, I'm going to divide you into two rides – A and B. Tomorrow, Ride A will go with Pete and myself for a picnic ride to Blueshell Bay, and Ride B, with Babs and Jackie and Paul, will visit the Home for Retired Horses at Birch Down. A minibus will call to take you there at 11 a.m.'

Babs and I looked at each other. The visit to the Home for Retired Horses would be super, but there had to be a snag. Why, oh why, had Sheila wished us on Paul, the grumpy twin?

'I suppose she thinks Paul may be able to keep us in order,' Babs sighed.

'Or she may want to give us the chance to

prove our pony-worth, and to redeem ourselves,' I said unhopefully. 'She's taking a
chance.'

'We're jinxed when Paul's around,' Babs
said feelingly.

Sure enough, next morning we were in the
camp kitchen putting up the picnic lunches
when Paul stormed in, and from that moment
things started to go wrong again.

'Aren't those sandwiches cut yet?' he demanded, when he saw that Babs and I were
still slicing up bridge rolls, and inserting the
cheese and tomato filling. 'The minibus will be
here in ten minutes.'

'Don't you fret. We'll be ready on time,'
Babs assured him.

'Well, just see that you are,' said Paul, going
off to round up campers.

Then we happened to turn our backs on the
Primus for only a moment, to buckle up two
rucksacks of food, and the milk boiled over.
We had to sprinkle salt over the boiling-ring
to take away the smell, and add a tin of
condensed milk and a jugful of water to make
up the loss.

Impatient horn toots from the minibus had
already sounded before the milk had come to
the boil. We were keeping everyone waiting.

All fingers and thumbs, Babs and I managed somehow to fill four giant Thermos flasks and screw down the tops before Paul stormed in again.

'Aren't you ready yet?' he demanded.

'Coming. Oh, just a minute,' gasped Babs. 'We've forgotten the cups.'

'And not only the cups, I bet.' Paul said with a groan. 'We'd better check. Now you look in the rucksacks, Jackie, as I call out the items. Spoons?'

I nodded meekly.

'Sugar?'

'Yes.'

'Biscuits? Sandwiches? Cake? Coffee?'

'Check,' I said, relieved and hopefully looked up for approval. 'Nothing missing.'

'Oh, come on,' said Paul, impatient. 'I've never met such a zany pair.'

I sighed and said nothing. Paul just didn't want to like us. It was impossible for me to do right. However, we must keep the peace for the sake of Sheila and Pete. Why did Paul have to be so *difficult*? Life at the Pony Camp would be wonderful if only Paul could be as pleasant as Pete.

And if wishes were ponies, all the campers would be riding. Life was never completely perfect, and people were never quite as one expected or hoped them to be.

With these philosophic thoughts, I silently took my seat beside Babs in the back of the minibus.

CHAPTER FIVE

A HORSY DAY

I wasn't downhearted for long. The driver of the minibus was something of a comic turn. He had long curly hair and side-whiskers. He fancied himself as something of a pop singer, so the minibus echoed as he gave us his version of several hits.

We all joined in, except Paul, and it was a jolly party that alighted in the white-railed enclosure in front of a rose-covered farm which was the headquarters of Birch Down Home for Retired Horses.

Mrs Green, who was in charge, led us into a big field. There, standing nose-to-tail, under the the shade of a chestnut tree, was a group of retired horses. They broke off their dozing and fly-swishing and cantered across as Mrs Green called them. Another horse lifted his head from the stream where he had been drinking, and trotted over. More came from over the brow of the hill, and soon we were surrounded by old, but healthy-looking, and obviously happy, horses. They ranged in size from a big Clydesdale, with shaggy legs, big hooves and gentle eyes, to a white donkey who had mothered many foals and had finally been rescued from a fairground in her thirtieth year.

There were also two cobs from a scrap merchant, a retired race-horse, three pit ponies, four farm horses and three Fell ponies.

'Bess and Amber and Brownie aren't really old enough to be retired,' Mrs Green told us, patting the Fell ponies as they nuzzled her sleeve, 'but they belonged to a gentleman who directed, in his will, that he didn't want his ponies to be sold from pillar to post. They were in danger of being put down, so we were able to persuade the executor to let them come here.'

Mrs Green left us to go back indoors where she had letters to write. We wandered over the fields, and ate our picnic by the stream. We were feeding scraps to the retired horses when a cattle van rolled up, and stopped before the farm.

Interested, we went across to see what

might be in the van. As we reached the white rails of the farmyard, Mrs Green came through the front door.

'This will be Magic Moment, our latest rescue,' she told us. 'Come and see.'

We crowded round as the ramp was let down and we could see, in the dimness of the van, fetlock deep in straw, a tall grey horse. The light seemed to dazzle him for a moment, and he made no attempt to move.

'Come on, then,' Mrs Green coaxed, going into the van. She grasped his head-collar and led him down the ramp. 'It's all right. This is your new home.'

Magic Moment stood uncertainly while Mrs Green made a fuss of him. We scrambled under the rail to add our welcome. Then Paul grabbed my shoulder.

'Keep back,' he warned. 'Can't you see he's a thoroughbred? You'll upset him.'

'Actually he's three-quarter bred,' said Mrs Green, trying not to be surprised by Paul's outburst. 'And you're quite right, Paul. Perhaps it's best not to overwhelm him too soon. He's a hunt horse.'

'I suppose he was going to kennels to make meat for the hounds,' Babs said, shocked. 'How wicked.'

'Yes, that's how it was,' Mrs Green said quietly. 'We had a hard job to persuade the hunt committee to let us buy him, and he was quite expensive. Still, he's safe now. Let's see how he takes to his companions.'

She led Magic Moment into the field. He caught sight of the other horses, and neighed. Captain, the Clydesdale, who seemed to be the leader of the retired horses neighed back, and, ears sideways, advanced to challenge the newcomer.

We all held our breath while the two horses suspiciously walked towards each other. Magic Moment's ears were lying flat and this was a tense moment. One never knew just what would happen when strange horses were introduced to each other.

'Quiet, everyone,' warned Paul.

We watched anxiously as Captain scraped the ground with an off-fore. Magic Moment did the same. Heads lowered and quite close together, ears all ways, the two horses repeated this procedure several times. Then, Captain turned and walked back to the other horses with Magic Moment following. Apparently the introduction had been successfully performed. To our relief, all the horses, led by Captain, raced round the field, tails streaming, their coats glistening in the sunshine. The white donkey brought up the rear. Magic Moment had been accepted by the herd.

'Lovely,' said our pop-singer driver. 'This calls for a whip-round.' He produced 50p. 'Put that towards buying the next horse,' he told our hostess. 'Fancy folk making nice horses into dog's meat, and after they've served them faithfully, too. Heartless, some people are.'

We all felt in our pockets and added what spare money we could find.

'Five pounds, eighty-three pence,' said Mrs Green gratefully. 'I must give you a receipt, and I'll put this into the Buying Warboy Fund. Warboy's the next hunt horse that we're bidding for.'

'Five pounds eighty-three won't go far towards buying a horse,' Babs said. 'Still, I suppose it's a start . . . I know!' Her face lit up. 'I've just had an idea.' She turned to Mrs Green. 'You know that you said Bess and Amber and Brownie weren't really old enough to be retired?'

I crossed my fingers and looked at Paul who was frowning. No doubt he could guess what was coming next.

'Yes, dear,' Mrs Green said encouragingly.

'Well,' went on Babs, 'do you think they'd

enjoy doing a bit of light work in a really happy home for the next few weeks? The money that they earn could go to buying Warboy.'

'And it would be doing us and the Pony Camp a good turn,' I added, not daring to look at Paul.

'Would it?' asked Paul, his blue eyes smouldering. 'Well, you might have asked me what I thought about it.'

Mrs Green turned to him with a helpful smile. 'Yes, I'm sure Bess and Amber and Brownie would be all right with you. I know Sheila's very good with ponies; and I think Mr Danesbury would have approved. After all, they're not really going from pillar to post. They'll be back here in a month, and the change might do them good. They're young enough to enjoy a few outings, and they would be helping to pay for Warboy. What do you think, Paul?'

Paul was still frowning. He looked from Babs to me, and then across at Mrs Green.

'I think it's quite a good idea, Mrs Green,' he said with an effort. 'Thank you very much.'

'No need for you to hurry the ponies back to camp,' said Roger, the oldest of the other campers, as Paul, Babs and I went with Mrs Green to collect the Fell ponies' tack. 'We'll

45

be back long before you, so we'll be able to start getting the meal.'

'Yes, that would be fun,' said Wendy. 'I've longed to try my hand at camp cooking ever since I arrived. Just tell us what is on the menu.'

'We were planning to have chops, tomatoes and fried potatoes,' said Babs, 'but if you can't manage that, use one of the big tins of corned beef and make a salad.'

The campers rolled off in the minibus and we heard their voices, led by the young driver, float back in song through the open windows.

With Babs mounted on Brownie, Paul on Bess and me on Amber, we thanked Mrs Green and rode out of the main gate.

Amber played up right away. The excitement of leaving the farm and seeing the big world again went to her head, and she progressed sideways for the first half-mile. Then a car whooshed past and she tried to climb the hedge-bank.

'There, silly.' Shortening my reins, I put my hand on her neck to reassure her.

'You managed that quite well, Jackie,' Paul said, appreciative for once, and I felt overwhelmed. He was actually making an effort to be pleasant to me. Wonders never cease.

The road forked. The main road with its stream of holiday traffic led back to Sandbeach. The other route was a bridle path dwindling into a sandy track behind the dunes and over the rim of the downs.

'We'd better go this way,' said Paul. 'Then Amber won't have any traffic to upset her.'

Paul opened a gate, holding it while Babs and I rode through. Babs caught my gaze, and gave a pleased wink and a nod. I knew what she was thinking. Was Paul trying to be gallant, polite and friendly? Had we won him over after all?

We trotted along the sandy track, with an occasional sideways dance from Amber. Then we came to the downs, and the mare gave a buck as she felt the turf under her hooves. She was fighting the bit, eager to be off. I decided to let her gallop to take the tickle out of her feet.

Amber extended herself, her hooves thudding and flecks of foam appearing on her neck. I let her gallop up the hill, and then pulled her up. Now she was resigned to a walk.

I turned in the saddle; Babs and Paul were some way behind. They seemed only to be trotting, so I walked Amber slowly on and then reined up, waiting for them to draw level. Suddenly, down on the beach below, a line of riders came into view round the sandhills. They were our pony campers, returning from their picnic ride with Sheila and Pete.

Pete was riding Daydream, and, as I watched, he pulled the bay mare away from the others and cantered purposefully towards a row of breakwaters. He took them stylishly, one after the other, the bay rising effortlessly.

'Look,' I said as Babs and Paul came up. 'Perfect timing. Pete certainly can jump.'

Babs shared my enthusiasm, but Paul barely glanced towards his twin. Annoyance showed in his face as he said to me: 'You are a clot, galloping off like that, Jackie. Amber was too fresh.'

'I thought it would be best to let her work off her excitement,' I tried to explain, but Paul cut me short.

'You were galloping wildly, out of control. Amber might have put her foot in a rabbit hole and broken her neck. Besides, your gallop might have upset Bess and Brownie, and started them playing up.'

I bit back a retort. It was no use arguing with him. He was his old grumpy self again. Silently I looked at him.

Paul's good-looking features were marred by anger. He was glowering towards the beach where his twin, having turned Daydream, was now riding back again over the breakwaters.

Paul dropped his gaze away as though for some reason he could not bear to look.

'What's wrong, Paul?' asked Babs in her most sympathetic tone. 'I know you're not upset simply because Jackie galloped Amber. There's some other reason. What is it? You can tell us.'

'Oh, shut up!' Paul's voice was taut. He spun his pony round. Then he said in a strangled tone, 'Come on. Let's get back to the camp now. And remember – no more galloping!'

CHAPTER SIX

THE HIDDEN TRUTH

'Just listen to the rain,' said Babs as we lay in our sleeping-bags under canvas that night.

Patter – patter – patter.

'A belt of heavy rain will sweep across Britain from the west particularly affecting coastal areas,' I quoted the weather forecast that we had heard on Roger's transistor during supper. 'Thank you and *good night!*'

We snuggled down, and I fell asleep to be wakened some hours later by Babs tugging at my shoulder.

'Something's happening,' said Babs. 'Listen.'

Above the sound of the downpour we heard voices. There was the flash of torchlights, and someone called:

'We're flooded out, too.'

'Trouble!' sighed Babs as we dressed and put on macs and wellingtons. 'I wonder whether Paul will blame us for this.'

Sheila and the twins were already coping with the emergency. Two tents were standing in several inches of boggy water, and the groundsheets were afloat in one of them, while a tin of talc was drifting down the field in a rivulet of muddy water.

'You can't stay here,' Sheila told the rained-out campers. 'Come across to the house, and we'll dry you out, and make up a couple of beds. Pete and Paul and Babs and Jackie will bring your kit.'

She shone her torch round at the other campers. 'Is anybody else's tent flooded?'

'Ours is worse than this one,' said a mousy-haired boy with spectacles.

'Then you'd better come across to the house, too,' said Sheila. 'How many are there of you, Micky? Six?'

Sheila led the flood victims to the farm, while the twins, Babs and I, equipped with torches, floundered through the muddy dark, salvaging the campers' belongings.

Soon after dawn, the twins, with the help of the boy campers, re-pitched the tents higher up the field. Then they all grabbed spades, and working in a row, sliced a ditch out of the muddy ground to drain away the water.

After lunch the rain became torrential.

Babs and I looked helplessly at Sheila. 'What are we going to do with the campers?' Babs asked.

'Well, this afternoon's taken care of,' Sheila told us, 'because Major Johnson, of the Pony Club, has promised to bring across his screen and projector and show some pony films.'

'What about tonight?' I asked.

'That's where you two can help,' said Sheila. 'Pete and Paul have got a portable cassette player, so I thought we might have dancing in the barn. I wonder if you could jolly it up a bit, put up some decorations and make it look festive.'

'Cross stirrups and stable brooms,' enthused Babs, catching on to the idea. 'Leave it to us, Sheila. We'll have a ball.'

Just then Sheila caught sight of Major Johnson's estate car through the window. 'I'll have to go and welcome our speaker now. You'll find some string in the top drawer of the dresser, and I think there are some old Christmas decorations in the corner cupboard.'

Leaving the campers to enjoy the pony films,

Babs and I raced off to the stables and, borrowing a couple of brooms, began to sweep out the barn with a will. We'd make this a dance to be remembered. Sweeping finished, we fixed a crossed broom and stable rake above the door, and another in the middle of the far wall. Then we tacked up stirrup irons to form a horseshoe with a broom and rake at the top. Underneath we placed an upturned stable barrow to serve as a table for the music, and flanked it with water buckets upside down.

We used half-full hay nets and well-polished bridles to decorate the side walls, and we dragged out the old piano, too.

'Now for the old Christmas decorations,' said Babs, starting off towards the farmhouse kitchen. 'I hope there are some streamers.'

Brushing the raindrops from our macs, we went into the kitchen. The whirr of the projector in the living room, and Major Johnson's voice explaining the forward seat, made a background with the rattle of rain against the window panes as we opened the corner cupboard.

'Oh, good – red and green streamers.' Babs's eyes lit up as she hauled them out. 'Cotton wool snowballs – no, they're too wintry. But those artificial fir branches will do nicely. Now for some string.'

I pulled open the drawer of the dresser. My gaze fell on a pile of gymkhana rosettes – ten or twelve red bearing the legend FIRST PRIZE, three or four blue, and one yellow.

'Just the thing.' I lifted them out. 'We can nail these on the rafters. They'll give a real pony atmosphere. Wait a minute.' I jerked the drawer forward. 'There are some more here.'

Two of the rosettes were wedged in the drawer at the back, so I lifted it out. As I did so the door of the cupboard underneath swung open and I caught a glimpse of a large silver cup.

'Goodness!' Babs pushed past me to inspect the trophy. 'If we polish this up, it'll look super. It's simply enormous. We might fill it with fruit cup.'

There were also some smaller cups. We lifted them out and placed them on top of the dresser, while we searched in various drawers for dusters and silver polish. They would make a wonderful set-piece for the pony dance.

'Fancy the Waynes winning all these,' I said, 'and not telling any of us.'

'These trophies definitely ought to be on display,' said Babs. 'They'd be a good advertisement for the Pony Camp.'

Suddenly I felt a draught on the back of my neck. I turned from the sink drawer where I had found the silver polish, and saw one of the twins standing in the doorway watching us.

Pete or Paul?

'What do you think you're doing?' The boy's eyes flashed as he glared from us to the cups and rosettes. Paul! 'Prying into our belongings, I see.'

'Hey, take it easy, Paul,' I protested. 'We're only looking for things to decorate the barn for the dance.'

'And these cups and rosettes are just the thing,' added Babs.

'Put them all back,' Paul ordered, and he looked so angry that I could picture him throwing them through the window.

'What's wrong?' I asked. 'Sheila told us to look for decorations for the dance, and these are absolutely super. Why hide them away? I should have thought you'd have been proud for people to see them. I would if I'd won all those.'

'So might I, if I had won them,' said Paul bitterly. He turned away, adding testily: 'Not that it's any business of yours.' He paused, and then said over his shoulder. 'Oh well, you may as well go ahead and use them. I can't stop you now.'

As Paul stalked away, Babs and I examined the cups.

PETER WAYNE
Under-16 Jumping – Open Championship Event
Fairlea Country Show

We looked from the big cup to the smaller ones. Peter Wayne Junior Jumping Competition. Peter Wayne under-14 pony trials. Peter Wayne under-16 one-day event.

'These are all Pete's,' I said, in surprise. 'None of them were won by Paul, nor even by Sheila. And I bet Pete won all those rosettes, too.'

Babs nodded. 'He was jumping marvellously over those breakwaters when we saw him on the beach yesterday.' She broke off, her eyes wide as at last she understood. 'So that's why Paul is so difficult. He's jealous of his twin – stark, staring *jealous*!'

CHAPTER SEVEN

SHOW-DOWN

Yes, Paul was jealous. I could see it all now. He couldn't bear the sight of other people being jumpers. That was why he'd been so angry when Pete had let me jump Daydream bareback, and why he'd been enraged at the sight of Pete jumping the breakwaters.

Babs and I voiced our thoughts as we got the refreshments ready for the barn dance.

'Pete and Sheila must have put the cups out of sight,' said Babs. 'I bet they thought it would be tactless to have them on display.'

'Gosh, yes!' I said, and added in alarm: 'And now Pete's cups are going to be on show tonight for everyone to see. I don't think we ought to have set them out.'

'Paul said we could,' said Babs.

'Yes, I know. But anyone could see that he really hated the idea.'

'Well, we can't put them back in the cupboard now without everyone asking a lot of questions,' said Babs. 'And then Paul will feel even worse.'

We speared sticks into some chippolata sausages. 'Somehow, Babs,' I said forebodingly, 'you and I just can't do right. There'll be ructions tonight over those cups, I know it.'

'How do you like Pete's pots. Jolly good, aren't they?'

I could hardly believe my ears. Those words were actually being spoken by Paul – the so-called jealous twin. He was standing by the display on a long table in the barn and speaking to the pony campers as they flocked in for the dance.

I listened in amazement.

Then I realized that Paul's words sounded carefully rehearsed. He was trying to be a good sport, trying to hide his jealousy. His smile was stiff, and his manner tense.

Just then Pete came into the barn, and Paul seemed to fade right into the background.

'Congrats, Pete,' said one of the girl campers named Cilla.

'A real show-jumper amongst us – what a thrill,' said the girl named Wendy. 'And we never knew.'

'What about entering for the Springfield Show, Pete?' put in Roger.

'I think you'll be in the White City class one day, Pete,' said another boy. 'How about giving me your autograph?'

Pete smiled, and chatted about his jumping triumphs, but I could see he was looking uneasy. After a moment he glanced round the barn for his twin. Then his smile faded. I followed his gaze and saw Paul, shoulders hunched, leaving the barn.

I felt so sorry for Paul. He'd made a big effort to be a good sport. Only Babs and I knew how hard he had tried to keep it up. Then, seeing everyone hero-worshipping Pete was too much for him. To show-jump must have been Paul's most cherished ambition; and he had probably found he was a duffer at it, while Pete was brilliant. That must have been a dreadful disappointment – and it had sown the seeds for his growing jealousy. If only I could help him.

'Come on, Jackie – dance!' Mickey's voice broke into my thoughts, and as we danced, my anxiety for Paul faded into the background for a while.

Then, three dances later, Babs grabbed my arm to remind me of a pony job that we had to do. Magpie had caught a chill, and just before the dance we had mixed him a bran-mash. Now was the time to give it to him.

As we hurried from the barn, I was reminded of Paul's earlier departure, and I looked around. I couldn't see him among the dancers. So he hadn't come back. What was he doing? Brooding, all alone in his room? Couldn't anyone do *anything* to make him feel happier?

Then Babs's voice dragged me back to the job in hand.

'It's just right,' she announced, removing the sacks from the bucket of mash. 'The mash has kept warm, but it's not too hot. Magpie's going to love this.'

We carried the bucket to the piebald's loosebox. The pony was standing there, sorry for himself. His ears pricked when he heard the clatter of a bucket, and soon he was lipping up the tasty mash.

Babs and I stayed with him until he had finished eating and started to doze. Then we crept out, closing the loosebox door. Strains of music wafted across to us from the barn.

'My favourite song,' said Babs, hurrying. 'Come on.'

'Just a minute.' I paused, suddenly feeling that something was missing from my wrist. 'My watch has gone. I'd better go back and look for it.'

'Don't be long,' said Babs, still heading for the barn. 'See you.'

I shone my torch down on to the floor of the loosebox, taking care to keep it out of Magpie's eyes, and searched among the straw for my watch. There it was, just beside the water bucket. I picked it up. The strap had broken. I put it in my pocket and was about to slip quietly out again without disturbing Magpie when I realized that I was not alone in the stables. There was somebody else – in Daydream's box at the far end of the range.

A boy's voice was talking softly to Pete's mare.

'Oh, Daydream! What am I going to do?'

I stiffened, recognizing the voice as Paul's. So he must have been in the stables all the time that Babs and I were feeding Magpie. He'd lain low so he wouldn't have to be pestered by us. Then, because he thought he was alone once more, he was pouring out his heart to the pony.

'Pete's a fine jumper,' Paul was saying. 'And here I am a real coward over jumping.'

He broke off. What was he doing now? Patting the pony, pressing his cheek against her neck?

I held my breath. Paul was speaking again

'I wish I could jump you, Daydream. That would be like the old days, wouldn't it, girl? We had good times together, you and I, until – '

I put my fingers in my ears. Paul was pouring out his heart, telling Daydream all the things he couldn't tell to anyone else. And I was having to eavesdrop. Worse still – I was going to sneeze! The dust from the straw was tickling my nose.

I put a finger along my upper lip trying to ward off the sneeze – and I had to hear Paul again.

'Well, I've got it off my chest.' Paul's tone now sounded more cheerful – more like Pete's voice. 'I've made up my mind. I'll show Sheila and Pete that I'm not jealous. I'll tell Pete he must go in for the Springfield Show – and I jolly well hope he gets some more pots.'

The sneeze was building up. I fought to suppress it. I was winning. The moment of danger was over. I relaxed and breathed again. Then – 'Atishoo!'

'What's that?' Paul's voice was edgy as he came into Magpie's box. 'Who's there?' His torch shone full on me as I tried to rush from the stables. 'Jackie!' Paul threw himself against the stable door, barring my escape. 'What are you doing here? You came back to hear what I was saying.'

'No, Paul, no.' I gasped. 'It's not like that. Really it isn't. Do let me explain. I dropped my watch and came back for it. Yes, I did hear what you said to Daydream. I understand everything now. Let me help.'

'Help?' Paul echoed. 'An interfering, scatter-brained girl like you? You and your nit-witted cousin! You're a pair of pests. I'm fed up to the teeth with you. Go on. Get back to the dance.'

He flung the door open.

'I'm not going,' I said 'until you've heard what I've got to say. I know why you're being angry with me. But I'm glad I overheard you, because now I understand. And I think it's terrible that you've got no one except Daydream to tell your troubles to.'

Paul's eyes smouldered. 'Are you going to go, Jackie, or do I have to throw you out?'

'Please listen, Paul,' I begged. 'You told Daydream that you weren't going to be jealous any more. Don't go back on that. I couldn't help hearing what you said, but I promise I won't breathe a word to anybody. Not even to Babs.'

'I don't care who you tell,' Paul challenged.

'Oh, yes, you do. You'd hate it. You feel humiliated because I heard what you said to Daydream. That's why you're so angry now. And I think it's such a shame – just when you'd made up your mind you were going to overcome your jealousy and help Pete to bring credit to the Pony Camp.'

'Shut up!' Paul's voice was curt. 'I don't want to hear.'

'I dare say,' I insisted. 'People don't like to face up to the truth. Yet you faced up to it when you were talking to Daydream. Why slip back? It was horrible for you that I should overhear it all, but it's not the end of the world. Lots of brothers get jealous of each other. Sisters, too – and cousins. Look, I *understand*. I don't blame you. You probably had some bad luck that spoilt your jumping chances. Why don't you tell me all about it? You might feel better then.'

'You'd be the last person I'd tell anything to.' Paul's voice was cold. 'Do I have to spell it out to you, Jackie? You're a P-E-S-T – a prying meddling *pest*. And so is your cousin. The best turn you could do me would be for you and Babs to pack up your kit and go. Go on! Get out! Out of this stable, and out of the Camp!'

CHAPTER EIGHT

A NOTE FROM PAUL

I fled from the sound of Paul's angry voice.
I didn't go back to the dance in the barn. I
couldn't face the lights and the music and the
carefree dancers. I felt miserable as I ran to
the camping meadow.

In the gloom of the tent I threw myself on
the air mattress and sobbed. Everything had
gone wrong. I'd failed. Instead of helping Paul,
I'd humiliated him; and now he didn't want to
see Babs or me again. We'd have to leave the
camp. It would be impossible to stay here with
Paul hating us, and to know that every time he
saw us his pride would be hurt afresh.

If I'd been in his shoes I'd have felt the same.
This was dreadful. I couldn't unburden myself,
not even to Babs. So when she came back
to the tent I pretended to be asleep. Then,
when Babs asked, 'Are you asleep, Jackie?' I

couldn't keep up the pretence and I blurted out: 'Oh, Babs, something terrible's happened. I can't explain. I promised not to. The fact is: we can't stay here any longer. We've got to go tomorrow.'

'It's something to do with Paul, isn't it?' Babs quickly sensed the truth. 'You've been crying. Has he been horrid to you? Why should we take any notice of him? We can't just go. We should be letting Pete and Sheila down. It's stupid?'

'Stupid or not,' I said unhappily, 'we can't stay here.'

Babs and I argued late into the night. She couldn't understand why I couldn't explain. We'd never had secrets before. She thought I ought to tell her, to trust her.

I suppose we fell asleep while we were still arguing, because suddenly it was morning and sunlight was glowing through the canvas.

I looked at my watch. Half-past six.

'Come on!' I shook Babs awake. 'We're making an early start. We've got to pack our kit, get Misty and Patch, leave a note and ride home.'

'Oh, go back to sleep,' groaned Babs.

I sat on my cousin's sleeping-bag, and grasped her by the shoulders. 'Now listen,

Babs – ' I would have to tell her everything after all. Then I broke off, listening. I could hear the swish-swish of gumboots in the dew-wet grass. Somebody was coming towards the tent. A shadow loomed over the canvas.

I held my breath, and signalled to Babs not to say anything.

'Jackie!' I heard Paul's voice from outside. 'Are you awake?'

I tried to make my voice steady as I said: 'What do you want?'

'Read this,' said Paul in a strained tone.

Paul's hand was thrust under the flap and I took a piece of paper from him.

As I opened the note I heard the thud-thud of his departing footsteps.

'What's it say?' Wide-awake now, Babs craned forward. We blinked and read:

You needn't go. It wouldn't solve any-thing. Pete and Sheila would only want to know what had happened, and so would the campers. It would lead to a lot of questions and fuss. Besides, we need your two ponies. If they went we'd be two mounts short. So you'd better stay after all, but please, Jackie, stop interfering and let me have a bit of peace. I've got to work

*things out for myself in my own way, and I
can only do that if you and Babs keep out
of my hair.*

Paul

'Well, that's a relief – our not having to go
after all,' said Babs. 'All the same, I think it's
a cheek. Paul wants us to stay because it would
make things awkward if we went. Yet at the
same time he's telling us to keep out of his way.
He hasn't considered our feelings, has he?'

I sighed. I didn't want to condemn Paul. We
didn't know all the circumstances. Sheila and
Pete hadn't told us, and why should they? It
seemed that it was none of our business. All
the same, when someone was unhappy and
beset with problems as Paul was, I couldn't
help feeling that someone had to do *something*
to help. If only we *knew* more so that we could
understand, and try once more.

'Oh, stop brooding about Paul.' Babs broke
into my thoughts. 'There are other people in
this camp, you know.'

Be busy – that was the way to stop brooding
I thought, and there was certainly plenty to
do. We cooked breakfast, packed the lunch
rucksacks, and helped the campers brush

their mounts, pick out hooves and saddle up. Misty gave me a puzzled look when Cilla rode her through the farm gate. With Magpie out of action, there wasn't a mount for either of the twins, and so they had to be left behind with us while Sheila rode Daydream.

'Come on,' Pete said as the hoof-beats died away. 'Let's see to Magpie and square up the camp. Then we can follow them. We've got four bikes.'

Magpie still had a cough. We gave him plenty of fresh water, greens and hay, deciding that Sheila would no doubt steam him that evening if necessary.

'You just snooze quietly, Magpie,' I told him, shutting the loosebox door. I was uneasy about leaving him, but I told myself that there wasn't much that we could do for him if we stayed.

Babs and I cut up the sandwiches for the boys and ourselves, and I was rather surprised that Paul had decided to come with us. He mumbled 'thank you' as I handed him his rucksack. Then he streaked off on his bike way ahead of us.

Even Paul's grouchiness could not dampen our spirits. Pete was his usual cheery self, and Babs and I felt our hearts lighten as we freewheeled down the winding hill from the headland. Paul was out of sight and out of mind for the moment.

We threaded through the Sandbeach traffic. Just ahead of us trotted a procession of donkeys, bells jingling, on their way to the sands.

The tide was on the ebb, and there was a splash of paddlers at the sea's edge. Passing the donkeys, we left Sandbeach and the promenade and turned along a honeysuckle-scented lane that led to Newberry Warren, with its bird sanctuary and forestry plantation of young trees.

We were on our way to Shell Island, an islet that was linked at low tide by a causeway to the mainland. As we breasted the hill, we could see it ahead of us beyond sandhills, rocky coves and a white-washed 'pepper-pot' of a disused lighthouse. The road led to a track through the dunes that had been planted with stands of young firs. Soon we had to dismount at a padlocked gate.

'We'll soon be there,' said Pete, gallantly lifting our bikes over the gate. 'You're going to like Shell Island. It's a real paradise.'

Small blue and brown butterflies flitted among the sandhills, and bees hummed among the tall, bright blue flower spikes of the wild anchusa that grew in clumps beside the track. We passed stands of fire-beating shovels, and Pete pointed out to us a watch-tower, built on stilts and roofed with pine branches. It was a lookout from which the forestry patrol could watch over the acres of young trees, and so instantly notice any outbreaks of fire caused by careless smokers or picnickers or, for instance, by broken glass intensifying the sun's heat and setting fire to dried wood.

'Oh, look!' I exclaimed when a biggish bird with long down-curved beak flew from the marram grass ahead of us, trailing its wing. 'A curlew. Poor thing, it must be hurt.'

'That bird's only pretending to be hurt,' said Pete. 'It's trying to fool us.' We stopped to watch the curlew flutter a little way ahead, and then droop its wing. 'Its nest must be near and it's trying to lure us away from the chick curlews.'

We trundled our bicycles along the track, enjoying the sweet scent of the yellow tree lupins that had been planted, with sea buckthorn and dwarf willow, to bind the dunes so that the sand would not blow away during gales. At the side of the track, tiny wild pansies, purple and white and gold, starred the sand.

Soon we came to the causeway, a stony

embankment, seaweed-strewn and mussel-encrusted. It stretched for a quarter of a mile from the shore to Shell Island.

We shielded our eyes from the sun-glare and watched some black-headed sandwich terns swooping, fork-tailed and swallow-like, to dive into the sea after fish.

We crossed the causeway and felt a thrill as we stepped on to Shell Island, with its beach blue-tinged by the crushed shells of mussels. Treading short turf spangled with the magenta of wild geraniums, we reached the top of the island. A gentle ridge with rocky coves sloped to tidepools. On our left lay a row of whitewashed coastguard cottages and the old lighthouse.

The Wayne ponies, now unsaddled, were tied to the fence in front of the cottages, and we could see the campers splashing and swimming in the bay. I saw a red-headed boy among the swimmers – Paul. He was doing a good crawl stroke, and I felt pleased because, for once, he looked as though he was enjoying himself.

Leaving our bicycles by the coastguard cottages, we ran to the beach, changed into our swimsuits behind some rocks, and were soon splashing with the others in the sea.

After our bathe we let the ponies graze, keeping a watchful eye on them while we ate our picnic lunch. Then we split up to explore the island.

'Come back here, everybody, when you hear three blasts on the whistle,' said Sheila. 'We must leave here at two thirty sharp because of the tide. So be sure to listen for the whistle.'

CHAPTER NINE

DANGER ON SHELL ISLAND

Babs and I scrambled over the rocks. We discovered an old wreck in one of the coves, and picked sea-thrift that grew above the tideline. Then we sunbathed on one of the headlands, watching the waves lapping over the sand.

We must have dozed off because it seemed no time at all until we heard the whistle blast calling us back to the mainland. Everybody else had already assembled as we hurried towards the coastguard cottages, and Sheila was glancing anxiously from her wristwatch to the sea which was already creaming over the rocks on either side of the causeway.

Cilla came towards me, leading my pony, Misty, who whinnied softly in greeting when she saw me.

'Here, Jackie,' Cilla said, handing Misty's reins to me. 'You have a turn. After all, Misty is your pony, and it seems a shame that you've barely had a chance to ride her since we've been at the camp.'

Heather offered Patch to Babs. 'We don't mind cycling back,' she said.

Misty seemed pleased. She rubbed her head against my shoulder as I let down the stirrup leathers a hole, and got ready to mount.

'Hurry, Jackie!' Sheila urged. 'The tide's coming in fast.'

'Carry on,' I called, putting my foot in the stirrup. 'I'm coming.'

Misty was excited. She edged round in a circle, keeping me hopping on one leg as I tried to mount. By the time I was on her back, the campers were crossing the causeway. Hardly had I settled myself when Misty gave a playful buck. I felt the saddle shift under me.

Cilla hadn't tightened the girths. Misty must have used her old trick of blowing herself out when she was saddled, and Cilla, not realizing, hadn't walked her on a few steps and pulled up the girth-fastening another hole or two. By the time I had dismounted and pulled up the girth, the sea was swirling over the first few yards of the causeway. The water was deepening every moment. I reined up Misty, and rode her down the shingle path between the rocks to the causeway which was now fetlock-deep in water.

Not being able to see her foothold, Misty naturally gibbed.

'Go on, Misty.' I drove her forward with my legs. She stopped again. I clapped my heels into her. 'Come on, girl. What's the fuss? You've been in the sea before.'

Sweat broke out on Misty's neck, and she turned a rolling eye towards me. There was only one thing to do. I dismounted and, pulling the reins over her head, led her into the water.

Shivering, Misty hesitated at every step. The water was swirling round my knees as desperately I pulled her on.

'Go back!' called Sheila from the mainland, and I saw the campers gesticulating from the safety of the opposite shore. 'Don't risk it. Stay on the island until the next tide.'

Before I could turn Misty to go back she took another step forward. There must have been a hidden dip in the causeway because suddenly the water was up to my waist. I felt Misty plunge sideways. Hanging tightly to the reins, I was dragged with her, and then we were both in deep water, floundering against the current which was sweeping us away from the shore.

'Don't panic, Jackie,' shouted one of the

twins, and I saw a red-headed figure, in blue jeans, splashing through the water towards us. 'I'm coming.'

Next minute, my feet touched firm sand, and I realized that Misty and I had been swept on to a sandbank. We were safe, but not for long. Soon the racing tide would cover the sandbank and swirl us out to sea.

'Pete!' I gasped, as the red-headed boy struggled chest-deep through the water towards us. 'Thank goodness you've come. How are we going to get Misty ashore?'

By now, my pony and I were standing in the middle of the quickly disappearing sandbank. The red-headed twin scowled as he splashed through the shallows towards us, and my heart sank.

My rescuer was Paul.

'Of all the clots!' Paul groaned. 'Why didn't you go back when we told you?'

I tried to explain, but Paul wouldn't listen. Meanwhile the waves were now lapping right over the sandbank. Soon our temporary refuge would be gone.

'There isn't time for anyone to fetch a boat,' Paul grumbled. 'So there's only one thing to do. Get on to Misty's back and stay there, even if she has to swim.'

With Paul leading her, I rode Misty into the water. From the shore Babs, Pete and some of the others were wading out to encourage her.

'Come on, Misty, old girl!' Babs urged. 'Come here to us.'

Misty's nostrils were flaring as she followed Paul into the deeper water. She was terrified. Then I felt her strike out strongly beneath me while the water reached my knees. My pony was now swimming towards the shore.

'Good girl, Misty.' I patted her neck as she swam. A few more yards and I felt Misty's feet touch firm sand. 'You've made it!'

As we came out of the water everybody crowded round, making a fuss of Misty and congratulating Paul.

'Thanks, Paul,' I said feelingly. 'If it hadn't been for you, Misty would have been drowned.'

'You were terrific, Paul,' said Babs. 'Three cheers.'

'Well done, twin!' praised Pete.

'We were proud of you,' added Sheila.

'For he's a jolly good fellow,' sang one of the boy campers and everyone joined in.

Paul was the hero of the hour and he was actually smiling. For once he and not Pete was in the limelight. I was so glad for Paul's sake.

'Take off Misty's saddle and ride back to camp,' Pete told me. 'That will dry her off and warm her up.'

'And you must change into some dry clothes, Jackie. You too, Paul,' said Sheila. She looked round at the rest of the campers. Everybody was rather wet. 'The sooner we all get back to camp and brew up some hot chocolate the better.'

Back at the camp Sheila insisted on my handing Misty over to Pete to be rubbed down and rugged up while I changed into dry clothes. Then Babs and I hurried to the stables to see how my pony was faring. Misty was looking comfortable, pulling at her hay net, while Pete was rubbing her ears. She whickered as Babs and I entered the loosebox, and I could see that she was enjoying all the fuss.

'Sheila thinks she ought to have some gruel,' Pete said. 'There isn't any linseed soaked, but she could have oatmeal. Will you make the gruel while I see to Magpie?'

A moment later Misty heard Pete talking to the piebald in the other loosebox. Why was Magpie having a fuss? Misty gave a protesting rattle of her water bucket. She hadn't liked being just one of the riding ponies, and now that she was on her own again, and having a fuss with everybody doing things for her, she wanted to keep it that way.

'Don't be such a nuisance,' I told Misty. 'You've got to stay on your own for a little while, and it's no use banging that bucket. Babs and I are going to make your gruel and you'll just have to be patient until it's ready.'

We went to the feed-store. I put a couple of handfuls of oatmeal into a pail, and then took it to the tap and poured out a little cold water, stirring it. Meanwhile Babs went to the kitchen to heat up a gallon and a half of water in several big saucepans.

We were in the kitchen pouring hot water on to the oatmeal when suddenly I began to shiver.

I sat down weakly. 'I do feel peculiar,' I said. 'My legs are trembly.'

'It must be delayed shock,' said Babs, putting her cardigan over my shoulders. 'Sit there quietly while I make a cup of sweet tea. That'll pull you round.'

I put my head in my hands as the memory of my ordeal came back to me. I could feel again the dreadful helplessness when Misty and I were swept away in the water.

'It was terrible,' I said. 'Simply terrible. We might have been drowned and all because

I took such a silly risk, thinking I knew best and that I could get across the causeway in time. I just didn't realize the danger. I didn't know the water would be so deep.'

'It was agonizing for us to watch you,' Babs said in a heartfelt way. 'When Misty was swept into the current, it was all Pete and I could do not to race in after you, but Sheila pulled us back. You see it was Paul who made the first move, while the rest of us were still rooted to the spot with horror. Paul's reactions must have been quicker, and he kicked off his shoes and was dashing into the water before we could move.'

'Somehow I'd expected Pete to be the hero,' I said. 'Not Paul.'

'Well, Pete was going to dash after Paul,' Babs explained. 'Then Sheila grabbed him by the arm, and said: "Leave this to Paul. He'll be able to cope." I suppose she didn't want Paul to be outdone by Pete in everything. She knew that this was something Paul could do.'

'Of course,' I said, taking another sip of tea and feeling better now. 'That explains it. Sheila knew that Paul isn't scared of water, even though he's scared of jumping.'

'Yes,' said Babs. 'Sheila wanted Paul to have a chance to shine at something. In a way,

Jackie, you did Paul a good turn by giving him the chance to rescue you.'

'Did I?'

'You've given him a new self-respect,' said Babs. 'The campers had got fed up with him. They thought he was just a drag, being so bad-tempered, and sulking all the time. Then, when he rescued you, everybody was so relieved that they just rushed forward to cheer and I thought I'd help things along, so I said "Come on, everybody, Paul's a hero. Let's show him that we think so, and then perhaps he won't be such a grouch."'

'Babs – shush!' I warned, too late.

Her words trailed off as she saw the look of dismay on my face. While Babs was speaking, a shadow had fallen across the open doorway of the kitchen.

Paul was standing there.

He must have heard every word. He looked defeated and utterly humiliated. His expression suddenly tightened and he turned away.

'Oh, Paul,' Babs gasped in dismay. 'You weren't meant to hear – it wasn't like that. Really it wasn't. I didn't mean it. Now I've spoiled everything. I'd give anything not to have said it.'

Impulsively she ran after Paul. She grabbed

at his arm. He brushed her aside and strode to the stairs. With Babs hurrying after him he raced up them. I heard a door shut, and then Babs knocking.

I ran after them.

'Paul!' I called outside his bedroom door. 'Come back. It must have sounded horrid, but we didn't mean it like that. We only wanted to help to make you feel better.'

I knocked on the door. There was no reply. I turned the knob. We must talk to Paul. We must straighten things out. We couldn't leave him like this – hurt and humiliated yet again.

'Paul, I'm coming in,' I declared.

I tried to push the door open. It would not budge. Paul must be holding it.

'Please, Paul.' I rattled the knob. 'Let us come in and explain.'

There was a grating noise as the key turned in the door. Paul had locked us out. Babs and I stood helpless, staring at each other in dismay, listening for any sound and hearing nothing. That was what made us feel even worse – the silence.

CHAPTER TEN

MY WORST FEARS

I'll never forget how helpless we felt, staring at that locked door, listening to the silence, and knowing that Paul was on the other side, and so unhappy.

At last we walked away, defeated, and I don't think I've ever been so miserable. Everything, but everything, that Babs and I did seemed to make things worse for Paul. If only Babs hadn't been telling me the truth about the rescue just at the moment when Paul had appeared! What a lesson that was – not to talk about people, especially when there is the slightest risk of their overhearing.

The long day dragged by, and still Paul didn't appear. We didn't blame him for avoiding us. Then, when he didn't turn up for tea, nor come to the sing-song in the barn, I decided that I must try again to make amends. I would have another talk with him. If he snubbed me, well, that was that. At least I would have tried.

I looked around the camp, meadows and farmhouse. There was no sign of Paul. Was he still in his bedroom behind that locked door? I forced myself to go up the stairs.

The door was ajar. He wasn't there.

I hesitated on the landing. Where could Paul be? Had he perhaps again sought solace with Daydream? Would he be sitting on an upturned bucket, talking out his troubles with the pony? I steeled myself to go to the loosebox. Paul wouldn't thank me for intruding. That was sure. But I must do everything possible to try to straighten out the misunderstanding.

As I crossed the yard, I heard a sudden outburst of noise; buckets banging and rattling, a thudding on wood, and the scared whinny of a pony. Forgetting Paul for the moment, I ran into Misty's loosebox, and gazed in dismay at the sight of her overturned feed and drinking buckets and water flowing across the cobbles.

'You naughty pony!' I scolded. 'So you're playing up again, kicking your bucket and banging it. I suppose you must be jealous of Magpie and upset because I haven't been riding you.' I put my arms round her neck. 'Oh, Misty, you're still my pony. When the camp's over we'll be going back home together and everything will be like it always has been. But what made you whinny? Have you hurt yourself?'

I examined Misty's legs for any cut. She was unharmed. Then, from Magpie's box, I heard a trampling of feet and a squeal. Oh dear, yet more pony trouble! I left Misty and dashed into the sick pony's box. The piebald, with his foot through the handle of his feed bucket, was banging it up and down desperately with a dreadful clatter, trying to free himself.

'Magpie,' I sighed, grasping his head and trying to soothe him. 'Just keep still. There! Don't panic or you'll really hurt yourself.'

I managed to get Magpie to trust me. Ears back, he stood trembling while I lifted his fore-foot and removed the bucket.

'I don't know what we're going to do with you and Misty,' I told him. 'You do seem to upset each other. I suppose I'll have to put Misty in the other stable where she won't be able to hear you. It's only for tonight. She's none the worse for her wetting, so she'll be able to go back tomorrow.'

From my pony's loosebox came an indignant whinny. Misty wanted to know why I was spending so much time talking to Magpie. She wanted all the love that was going, every bit of it, all to herself.

'Please be patient, Misty,' I called. 'I'm coming, but there's something else I want to do first.'

Foremost in my mind were thoughts of Paul. Was there a hundred to one chance that he might be in the end loosebox, silently waiting for me to go away?

'Paul?' I called breathlessly as I peered through the dusk into Daydream's box. 'Are you there?'

I stopped in surprise. Paul was not in the loosebox – nor was Daydream! Where was the pony? It was just possible that Pete might have put her in the field with the others. He might have decided to let her have a restful day. I hurried to the field.

In the falling darkness I ran from one sleeping group of ponies to another, checking them all. Pete's mare was not among them. Daydream was missing, and so was Paul.

What did that mean? What ought I to do? Tell Sheila and Pete?

I ran to the barn. The lively music was a contrast to my desperate mood. Sheila was thumping away at the piano, but I managed to corner Pete who had paused in his mouth organ playing to grab a lemonade.

'Not to worry,' Pete said, calmly. 'Paul's probably gone for a ride.'

'You don't understand,' said Babs. 'Paul hasn't just gone for a ride. I think he may have run away. He was upset. Something rather dreadful happened.'

Pete looked serious as we told him everything. He consulted his watch. 'It's a quarter-past nine now. When did you last see him? Six or so?'

I shook my head. 'He wasn't in to tea.'

'No,' agreed Pete, 'he wasn't. But I didn't think anything of it. I suppose I thought that Sheila might have given him his tea in the house as soon as he'd got dry and changed after the rescue. I wonder how long he's been gone?'

'Hey, Pete,' said Cilla who had dashed across the barn. 'The music's nothing without your mouth organ.'

Pete forced a smile, shrugged off his worry and wiped his mouth organ on the sleeve of his pullover. 'Perhaps Paul will turn up any minute,' he told me. 'Don't flap. I'll have a word with Sheila as soon as this number's over.'

Though his tone was light-hearted, I could

see that he was still worried. He put his mouth organ to his lips and began to play.

'Come on, Jackie.' A crinkly-haired boy called Rex came up to me, holding out his hand. 'Dance!'

I tried to throw myself into the spirit of the evening's jollity, although I was sure Pete was now having uneasy feelings about Paul. He was looking anxious. His eyes seemed strained while he played his mouth organ, and I noticed him glancing now and then towards the door as if to check whether his twin had returned. People say that twins can always sense when the other one is in trouble, and Pete was becoming more and more anxious every moment.

Presently he made an excuse to leave the barn, and I guessed that he was going to see if there was any sign of his twin.

Five minutes later he was back. He seemed really worried now. I watched him go across to Sheila.

'Just a moment, Babs,' I said to my cousin with whom I was dancing. 'Something's happening. And I think it's something to do with Paul.'

I pushed my way to Pete and Sheila in time to hear Pete say: 'He's taken his torch, and his sleeping-bag, and the saddle-bags have gone. I suppose he's also taken Daydream's ration of concentrates. I tell you, Sheila, he's running away. I know he is. I can feel it.'

'Paul wouldn't cause us all this worry,' said Sheila. 'Surely he'd have left a note. Perhaps he has, and we haven't found it. We'd better search.'

'Shall I help?' I asked.

'Thanks for the offer, but no,' said Sheila. 'You and Babs go to the kitchen and make some cocoa. It's time the campers were getting to bed. Some of them are going home tomorrow and they've got a long journey ahead of them.'

In the kitchen Babs put on the milk to boil and filled the electric urn with water while I set out the mugs.

I stood on tiptoe by the shelf to reach down the drinking chocolate and biscuit tin. As I did so I noticed a piece of paper lying upside down on the floor at my feet. It must have been propped on the shelf, and then blown down. I picked it up and saw, on the other side, in Paul's handwriting:

Dear Sheila and Pete – You don't need me around. The camp will get by without me, so I'm going to Gran's – Paul.

Babs and I re-read the note, our worst fears confirmed. Paul must have felt that he couldn't face us again, especially after overhearing what Babs had told me she'd said to the other campers after the rescue. Probably he felt that everyone was laughing at him.

'He can't hope to get to his granny's tonight,' Babs said, 'because Sheila was talking about her the other day and she lives at Dorrington.'

'That's twenty miles away,' I said. 'Sooner than wait until tomorrow, Paul set out tonight. That's why he's taken his sleeping-bag. He must have felt that he just couldn't face spending another night in the camp. And it's all our fault. I feel dreadful.'

CHAPTER ELEVEN

IN SUSPENSE

We were in the kitchen, boiling milk for the campers' night-time cocoa, when Sheila telephoned Granny Wayne. The old lady was slightly deaf, which in a way was lucky for us, because she spoke loudly and we could hear almost every word as we stood near the telephone.

'But what's wrong, Sheila?' Granny Wayne asked. 'Of course I don't mind Paul coming here. But he hasn't let me know. I suppose he might have telephoned when I was in the garden and I didn't hear the bell. But surely he's needed at the camp now. He ought to be helping you and Pete.'

Then Sheila told her grandmother what had happened.

'What a pity,' came the old lady's voice, 'just when we wanted everything to go smoothly for Paul, so that he could get his confidence back.'

I winced. The family had been counting on things going right for Paul at the camp; then Babs and I had ruined it all.

We could hear the Waynes' grandmother adding: 'Paul must learn to face up to his problems. Running away won't solve anything. Ah well, I'll ring you tomorrow as soon as he arrives. Try not to worry, dear.'

To add to our problems, tomorrow, Saturday, was change-over day, the busiest day of the week. Everything was rush – rush – rush!

We had to say goodbye to the campers who were departing. We swopped addresses and helped them with their kit. Then, almost immediately, we were welcoming the newcomers. We settled them into their tents and introduced them to each other. Then we asked two of the campers who were still here from the previous week, to take the newcomers to the meadow to meet the ponies, while Babs and I prepared a salad lunch.

Pete and Sheila ate their lunch in the kitchen to be near the telephone, but Babs and I had to take the salad and sliced ham across to the marquee for the hungry campers. After the meal Cilla and Heather and a friendly new boy named Tony offered to do the washing up, so we went with them across to the kitchen to fill their buckets with hot water.

'Any news?' Babs asked as we went indoors.

Pete shook his head, and his blue eyes looked troubled. 'Sheila's just telephoned Gran again. Paul still hasn't arrived. Of course he might have stopped on the way for any number of reasons. Daydream might have cast a shoe. We're going to give him until three o'clock and then, if he still hasn't arrived, we'll have to start searching.'

We had to wait around the camp all day, and so, to keep the campers happy, we arranged some easy jumps in the field. Patch and Bess were jumping in style, and their riders managed to stay on, although Heather was once thrown on to Patch's neck.

With Cilla riding her, Misty cleared the jumps twice before refusing when she saw me watching, as though to say: 'Why have you forsaken me?'

I walked over to the gate where Babs was waiting.

'No need to offer you a penny for your

thoughts, Babs,' I said, seeing how pensive my cousin was looking.

'I can't get Paul out of my mind,' said Babs. She looked at her wristwatch. 'Three o'clock was Sheila's deadline, and now it's five past'

Just then came the reedy sound of a hunting horn – Pete's signal to summon the campers together. Babs looked at me in alarm and said: 'That means there's no news of Paul. This is an emergency. Look, there's Sheila. She's beckoning us to the stable-yard.'

As we reached Sheila and Pete, we could see that they were really worried, although Sheila was trying to keep her voice steady while she briefed the searchers.

'We're going to look for Paul,' she announced. 'Now we'll need some of you to stay behind. Micky, would you be on telephone duty, ready to take any messages? And you, Heather, if you'd stay with him so that you can ride and let us know if any news comes through. Then we'll need two more people to meet the other campers when they arrive and to see that they're fed and settled in.'

'Pam and I will do that,' volunteered a new girl called Gladys.

'That leaves eight of you to search with us, then,' said Sheila. 'Are you all good riders?'

Babs and I looked round at the eight campers. There were Cilla and Wendy and Tony and five of the other newcomers all of whom had handled their ponies competently in the meadow.

'Paul should be somewhere between here and Dorrington,' Sheila told us. 'That's twenty miles away and he may have taken any one of four different routes. There are twelve of us altogether, so we can split into groups of three and each take a different way. Two of you come with me and ride through Sandbeach. Two go with Pete to the Downs Road. Two go with Cilla and follow the route through Low Cross and Minton. Babs and Jackie – take one camper with you and go cross-country. Keep your eyes open all the time, because Paul may have met with an accident.'

'And ask at all the smithies,' put in Pete. 'Just in case Daydream's cast a shoe.'

We collected packets of biscuits and apples from Pete before we mounted. Then, with Tony accompanying us on Bess, Babs and I rode out across the fields, following the bridle path to Marsham in search of Paul.

Misty was overjoyed to have me on her back again, but I couldn't share her joy. All my thoughts were of Paul. Where was he?

Why hadn't he reached his grandmother's? And when we found him – what then? It was obvious that he hadn't wanted any fuss. And now there was the biggest fuss of all – twelve riders out searching for him, tracking him down.

How was Paul going to feel about that? What would he do?

CHAPTER TWELVE

THE OLD WOMAN'S WARNING

'No, miss, I haven't seen hair nor hide of young Paul these last few days,' the blacksmith told us. 'Is anything wrong?'

'We don't know yet,' I explained briefly. Then Tony, Babs and I rode away from the forge through the main street of Marsham village. We turned down a green lane between banks of gorse. Presently the lane widened, and we came to a cottage. Through the open doorway we could glimpse an old woman sewing.

We reined up and Babs called to her: 'Please, can you help us? We're looking for a boy on a bay pony.'

'Would the pony have a black mane and tail?' she asked, coming down the steps.

'That's right,' I nodded.

'And would the boy have red hair?'

'Yes, yes.'

'And he'd be handsome, only he looked so worried.'

'That's Paul,' I said, definitely. 'Please go on.'

'Yes, I've seen him,' the woman declared. 'Last evening. He'll be well on his way by now.'

'Are we on the right track if we ride straight on?' I asked.

The woman nodded.

We turned our ponies, ready to take up the trail again.

'Wait!' the woman called after us. 'He was asking me where he might find somewhere to sleep. I told him there was an old barn about three miles on. To the right of the oak wood, it is. There's no farm near. Nobody there to disturb him. And I gave him some food. Well, I saw the lad were travelling light and I thought he might be needing something seeing he'd such a long way ahead of him.'

'A long way ahead of him?' Babs echoed with foreboding. 'How do you know?'

'Because I told his fortune,' the old woman said wisely. 'Not that there was much fortune in his palm that I could see, leastways not just yet.'

'That wouldn't make him feel any better,' said Tony.

'What else did you see in his palm?' asked Babs.

'Trouble!' said the woman. 'I could see trouble behind him. He was riding with trouble now, and there was trouble ahead. A blight had come into his life.'

Two blights, I thought miserably – Babs and me.

'But it wasn't all fate's doing.' The woman paused. 'Folk's fate isn't all written in the palm of your hand, nor in the stars. A lot of it's what you make it, and mark my words, that lad's at the cross-roads.'

'Oh good,' Tony said. 'Tell us precisely which cross-roads, so that we can gallop there and catch him up.'

'You may scoff, young man.' The old woman seemed to pierce Tony with her dark eyes. 'But heed what I do say. That lad's at the end of his tether, and you need to find him soon. He could go one way or the other, to trouble or to happiness, like the future of the other lad he's linked to.'

Goodness! I thought, suddenly convinced, she must really have sixth sense. She knew Paul was linked to Pete – a twin. Yet nobody had told her. What she was foretelling must be right.

'Where is he now?' I asked eagerly. 'Can't you give us any clue?'

'How can I tell you?' the old woman said. He's not here for me to see his hand. Let me see one of your right hands.' She looked at us in turn and her gaze met mine. 'Yours.'

I wiped my hand on my jeans before holding it out to her. The old woman stared at it for a moment and then said, 'Your fate crosses his by water not by land. That's all I can see.'

We trotted on. When we were out of earshot Tony chuckled scornfully.

'What a lot of rubbish!' he scoffed. 'If any fortune-telling ever does seem to come true, it's either wishful thinking, coincidence or clever guess-work.'

We rode for a little while. Then, sure enough, we came to the oak wood, just where the old woman had said.

At the edge of the wood stood a stone barn in a field of long grass. It seemed a forsaken place; no one would be likely to disturb Paul there. The door lay rotting among a thistle-patch, and dusty sunlight slanted through the doorway, showing up a jumble of hoof-marks on the earth floor.

'Paul must have tied Daydream to this ring bolt,' I said.

'Here's where he made a fire,' said Babs, searching around outside.

We gazed at the blackened circle of the raked-out fire where Paul had cooked a meal. Then we cast around for further clues.

'This is the way he went.' Tony pointed to the flattened grass at the edge of the field where Daydream had passed, girth-high.

We followed Daydream's track through the long grass. We lost it when we came to the next field.

'He could have gone any of three different ways,' said Babs, looking at the public footpath sign which pointed towards Tor Brow on the one side, Brookbank on the other, and Golden Bay in between. 'We'll have to split up.'

'I'll go to Golden Bay,' I volunteered, thinking of the old woman's words: 'Your fate crosses his by water not by land.'

'Meet later at Market Cross,' Babs suggested.

'See you,' I called and split up.

I put Misty over the stile and cantered her along the shady path at the edge of a spinney. We jumped another stile and came on to the downs. Misty tossed her head.

'Thank you for letting me be your pony again,' she seemed to say.

Her hooves thudded joyfully on the thyme-starred turf. Strangely I felt a sixth sense of my own – that we were galloping headlong to something that was written in our fates, Paul's and mine. Good or bad? I didn't know which.

'By water,' the gipsy had said, and there, ahead of me, was the sea shining like molten gold in a V-shaped gap in the hills.

I turned Misty towards the gap, and the breeze rushed past us as we galloped. The path became narrow when we neared the sea. I was eager to press on, but I had to slow Misty to a walk.

We were riding down a shepherd's path to the sand dunes and the marsh. The sea was quite rough, and I could see the darkling shadows of the wind chasing over the water and whipping the waves into white cat's paws. A few hundred yards more and I could see the beach with the seagulls waiting at the tideline. A sense of foreboding came over me again. I shuddered as Misty gave a shrill whinny.

The sun emerged from a cloud, blazing on to the sea, dazzling me. I couldn't see anything. Then, above the cackles of the herring gulls, I heard the thud-thud of hooves on wet sand.

I shielded my eyes, blinked and looked ahead again to see the sun-blurred silhouette of a pony and rider cantering away from a low breakwater. I strained forward in my saddle. Just then a wisp of cloud filtered the glare of the sun at the exact moment that the rider turned his pony.

Now I could see him clearly, his light blue jeans, yellow jersey and ginger hair. I caught my breath, and my hands tightened on Misty's reins.

I had found Paul.

CHAPTER THIRTEEN

FACE TO FACE

Now that I had found him, what should I do?
What could I say?

I hadn't a clue. So many times I had done the
wrong thing and made matters a hundred times
worse. Fervently I wished that Sheila and Pete
were here, so that they could cope.

I sat low in the saddle, dreading that Paul
might catch sight of me before I had decided
what to do.

Then my dread turned to amazement as I
watched what Paul was doing.

He was practising jumping. Paul jumping! –
yes, the unbelievable was happening before my
very eyes.

I crossed my fingers for him to be lucky as
he put Daydream into a canter and rode her
at the low breakwater. He cleared it easily.
It wasn't a particularly high jump, but Paul

had flicked the show-jumper with his switch and taken it in style and with confidence. I did so want him to succeed. Suddenly my spirits soared. Paul need not be unhappy any longer. He was conquering his fear. This was wonderful. This must have been his plan, his secret hope, when he said that he wanted to solve his problems in his own way. He must have felt he could only start to jump again if he were far away from people, where no one could see him if he failed.

What should I do? By suddenly appearing on the scene I might spoil everything for him yet again. I decided to ride quietly away, and go to find Sheila and Pete. They might decide it would be best to let Paul carry on working out the solution to his problem in his own way. After all, he wasn't coming to any harm. He'd got the barn to sleep in, and I suppose he had money with him to buy food for himself and Daydream.

I watched, delighted for Paul's sake.

Now he was riding Daydream towards the next breakwater which was slightly higher, though still quite an easy jump. I sat frozen to my saddle so that he wouldn't see me. I would wait until he'd completed the jump. Then he would probably turn Daydream and ride her at the breakwater once more. His back would be turned to me. That would be my chance quietly to ride away. Paul's whole mind was set on the jump. His attitude was one of tense anxiety. His arms were stiff as he put Daydream at the jump.

'Please, Daydream,' I wished. 'Help Paul. Jump for him.'

Then Paul jabbed the pony's mouth. She stumbled on landing, throwing him on to her neck. He slid over her ears and sprawled on to the sand.

At that moment, my pony gave a high-pitched whinny. I suppose she was calling to Daydream, but, to Paul, it must have sounded a mocking sound.

This was dreadful.

I turned to flee. Misty wouldn't go. She was determined to join Daydream on the beach. She dug in her feet, stubbornly stiffened her neck, bucked and then climbed on to a sand dune. Paul scrambled angrily to his feet and glared at us.

'Jackie! What are you doing here?' His astonishment turned to anger and he shouted: 'No. Don't go. I want to know why you're spying on me again.'

My hands quivered on the reins as Paul

flung himself on to Daydream's back, clapped his heels into her sides and galloped straight towards me. I wished the sand would open and swallow me up. Paul reined to a skidding halt, and Misty stretched out her nose to greet Daydream.

I managed a nervous smile. Even that was a mistake. He thought I was laughing at him.

'Yes, very funny. Ha! Ha!' Paul's voice was sarcastic. 'Now you'll have something really amusing to tell Babs and the others. How long have you been watching? Why didn't you let me know you were there? I suppose you were waiting for me to fall off, so that you could have a horse-laugh!'

At last I found my voice.

'I wasn't laughing, Paul. I thought you were doing quite well.'

'Who are you trying to fool? Why, I couldn't even stay on over a two-foot breakwater! I suppose you think I'm such a fool that it was marvellous that I could jump anything at all, even a matchstick.'

'No, Paul, it isn't like that.'

'Isn't it?' Paul was shaking with anger. 'Well, I don't care how it is. I don't care what you think. I'm fed up with you. I was getting on fairly well before you turned up.

Then you had to spoil everything. What are you doing here anyway?'

I gulped. I'd have to tell him the truth.

'I'm one of a search party, Paul,' I explained. 'Everybody's looking for you. Sheila and Pete were worried when you didn't turn up at your gran's.'

'Search party?' Paul groaned. 'I tried to telephone twice, but the line was busy. I was going to telephone again when I rode into the village to get more food.'

'Listen, Paul.' I plucked up my courage. 'Why don't you come back with me to the camp?' I leaned forward to put a hand on Daydream's bridle. 'Everybody will be glad to see you.'

'I dare say.' Paul tried to snatch away the reins. 'Well I'm not coming and you can go back and tell them so. I'm off.'

'Please, Paul – '

'Don't you ever stop interfering?' He faced me. 'You've spoilt the whole camp and the whole summer for me. Just when I'm really trying to tackle things, you have to butt in again and ruin everything. You're a blight, a nuisance and a *pest*!'

I put my hands over my ears to blot out his words. Then suddenly I knew I couldn't take any more. It was now my turn to lose my temper.

'You're the most selfish, thoughtless, stupid boy I've ever met,' I rounded on him. 'You've got a wonderful sister and brother. They try to help you and to cover up for you, and to make a go of the camp, while you're always behaving like a bear with a sore head. You've spoilt things for the campers. You've never pulled your weight. You've only thought about yourself. You're jealous of Pete who's the best and most loyal brother any boy could have. He's worth twenty of you. You're just a millstone round his neck. You're suspicious and sulky. You're always sorry for yourself. You're just impossible. I hate you!'

I broke off, suddenly shocked by my own behaviour and the fact that Paul looked so completely stunned and silenced.

It was as though every word of mine had gone home, and he was realizing, for the first time, how his behaviour must have seemed to other people. He gazed at me, open-mouthed. Then a flush spread over his face. He gathered up Daydream's reins, wheeled her round, and galloped away, too upset to say a word.

What had I done? Now Paul might never again be able to face up to the pony campers not while he thought everybody was thinking horrid things about him.

'Paul,' I called, galloping Misty after him 'I didn't mean what I said. It isn't really like that. Everyone likes you. Everyone's sorry because you're unhappy.'

I broke off. Paul was thundering away, out of earshot.

Soon he reached the downs, and, crouching lower over Daydream's neck, galloping flat out as though he wanted to ride away from everybody and everything.

I urged Misty after him. On we sped over the turf of the downs. Once I lost sight of him when he and Daydream entered a hollow. Then he came into sight, breasting the rise on the other side.

'Paul,' I shouted. 'Please wait.'

If Paul heard, he gave no sign. He rode Daydream even faster, and only once looked back over his shoulder to shout a desperate plea: 'Go back, Jackie. *Leave me alone.*'

CHAPTER FOURTEEN

DISASTER – PLUS PAUL

'Faster, Misty, *faster*!'

I galloped after Paul as though my life depended on it. This time I must succeed in putting things right. It was now or never.

Daydream was well in the lead. With Paul crouched forward in the saddle, she raced up the hill to the top of the downs and then extended herself over the flat turf. Grass flew from beneath her hooves. Her tail streamed in the wind. Twisting between the gorse bushes, she crossed the sheep tracks, plunged down into a hollow and crossed a gulley to thunder up the hill on the far side.

Misty stumbled on some loose stones, throwing me on to her neck. I wriggled back into my saddle, patted her neck and urged her on again. Paul was far ahead of us now. He galloped behind some tall clumps of gorse.

I caught sight of him, twisting and turning Daydream among a patch of stunted thorn bushes. Then he was gone. Just as I thought I'd lost him, I caught sight of him again. He was heading straight for a shut field gate that led off the downs to a lane. He slackened his speed to a canter. This part of the downs was fenced.

'Faster, Misty!' I urged.

Misty was flat out as Paul, not able to face jumping the gate, slid off Daydream's back, opened it, and led her through, pushing the gate shut to check my advantage.

I pressed my heels into Misty's sides and put her at the gate. I knew it was too high for her, yet I had to take the risk. This was my only chance to catch up with Paul and make him understand that I hadn't meant the hateful things I'd said about him, that I'd just lost my temper.

'Up, Misty, *up*!'

The gate was high for Misty, though the ground was firm. She took it gamely, but touched it with her back legs in going over. She pecked on landing, and recovered. Then her back legs crumpled under her.

I jumped off in alarm.

'Misty, what's wrong?'

I bent to examine her. To my horror I saw blood gushing from a gash in her near-hind. There must have been half-hidden wire on the far side of the gate. Misty had caught her leg on it, cutting deeply into her flesh and gashing an artery.

'Paul!' I called desperately. *'Help!'*

Daydream's hoof-beats sounded fainter. Paul either hadn't heard my call for help, or he hadn't heeded it. Blood soaked through my hanky. I tried to wind it round Misty's hind leg above the gash, but it would not reach. It was tiny and useless.

Misty trembled, whinnying with pain. I pressed the blood-soaked hanky as tightly as I could to the wound. Still the blood flowed.

Oh, Paul! I thought desperately. If only you'd heard. If only you'd help. Then I was aware of Daydream's hoof-beats again. This time they were getting nearer.

Paul had heard. He was coming back. He wasn't leaving us in the lurch after all.

I looked up as he scrambled off Daydream.

'Trust you,' he groaned. 'Here, let me.'

He pulled off his belt, and as I soothed Misty, threw aside my blood-stained hanky, made the belt into a tourniquet and wound it round Misty's leg. He tightened it by putting his switch through the knot and twisting it to apply the extra pressure to seal off the severed artery and so stop the bleeding.

'Now, Jackie,' Paul said firmly, 'hold the tourniquet like this to keep up the pressure on the artery.'

'Yes, Paul.'

'Here's my watch. Slacken that tourniquet in twenty minutes. Then tighten it again. Don't forget. It's dangerous to keep it tight for too long. I'm going to try to get the vet.'

I tried to stop my hands shaking as I held the switch. Hoping that Paul would be back before the twenty minutes were over, I watched him mount Daydream and gallop down the green lane.

A gate and stile blocked his way. Paul wavered. He knew that precious moments would be wasted if he stopped to unfasten the gate.

I saw him hesitate for a moment. Then he steeled himself to put his pony at the stile.

Up, Daydream! I prayed.

Daydream jumped like a champion. I saw Paul nearly lose his seat, but he regained it, fumbled for his stirrup and galloped headlong down the lane.

Misty's eyes rolled and she tried to pull

away from me. I held her tightly, took off my jacket and put it across her quarters to stop her shivering.

'Misty, darling,' I murmured soothingly. 'You're the sweetest pony in the world.'

The minutes ticked agonizingly by on Paul's watch. Some sheep bleated on the downs, their lonely cries seeming to emphasize our plight. Misty was standing head down, eyes glazed, dejected. Ten minutes dragged by, then twelve, now fifteen. I watched a jet plane climb high in the sky, leaving a fleecy vapour trail. *Twenty minutes*. With fingers trembling I loosened the tourniquet, only hoping that I would be able to get it tight enough again. Blood spouted from Misty's wound, and I had to force myself not to panic as I waited for circulation to be restored to her leg.

Misty must have felt pain when the sensation crept back into her limb. She flinched and moved, and the bleeding seemed even more alarming. I twisted the tourniquet tight again, holding it there. Misty was uneasy now, and I had difficulty keeping her still.

Hurry, Paul! I prayed, trying to stifle the dread that Paul might be lying injured in a ditch having taken a too-risky jump for Misty's sake.

Then I heard the beat of cantering hooves. They quickened to a gallop, then paused for the take-off. I looked up to see Daydream, with Paul still in the saddle, arching over the stile in a perfect jump.

'The vet's on his way,' he called. He scrambled down from Daydream, tied her to the fence and ran to check Misty's tourniquet. He took the watch from me. 'I've been longer than twenty minutes. You loosened it, didn't you?'

I nodded.

'I rode to the vet's surgery at Little Marsham,' Paul told me. 'He was out on a call. His wife rang the farm that he was visiting, and I told him exactly where you were. He said he would finish treating a sick heifer and then he would come straight here.'

'Oh, Paul, I'll never be able to thank you,' I said fervently. 'You were super. You didn't lose a minute. You jumped that stile as if you never gave it a second thought.'

'I hadn't time to think,' Paul admitted. 'Daydream saw the stile ahead of her, and she just took charge. We were over almost before I knew what had happened. That's how I lost my stirrup.'

'Yes, I noticed,' I said. 'Then you were out of sight. What happened?'

'Well, I took another jump. It was only a post-and-rails. Then I put her over the gorse hedge. We jumped on the way back, too.'

I looked keenly at him. 'You know what this means don't you?'

Paul nodded. 'Yes, it seems that I might be getting my nerve back.' His eyes were bright with half-suppressed excitement. 'I shall make myself go on jumping now.'

He soothed Misty, and then glanced up as we heard a car approaching along a bumpy lane. Paul jumped on to a bank, and waved.

'We're over here,' he called to the vet, hurrying to open the gate. A moment later the vet was taking charge, and I knew Misty would be saved, thanks to Paul, the boy whom I said I'd hated.

'I don't want to be a pest, Paul,' I said quietly while the vet was busy with Misty, 'but you must listen for a moment.'

I could almost hear Paul mentally groan. I paused and went on, refusing to be deterred. 'I didn't mean a word of what I said when I was angry. Truly I didn't. None of it.'

Paul didn't answer. He looked down at the ground. I felt worried. Now the emergency about Misty was over, would Paul start

119

disliking me again? Would his former grumpiness return, and would I always go on hating myself for what I had said to him?

I kept my gaze on him. He brushed a gnat from his freckled cheek, scratched his ginger head, looked at me straight in the eyes and sighed.

'You never give up trying, do you, Jackie?'

I shook my head.

'And you know that trouble is always one step behind and one step ahead of you. You realize you're a real jinx, don't you?'

'I suppose so.'

'But then,' said Paul, and suddenly his tone lightened, a smile curved the corners of his lips, and the sunlight was reflected in his blue eyes – 'then if you hadn't been disaster-prone, you wouldn't have got yourself and Misty into this spot of trouble.'

'No, Paul,' I admitted. 'That's true.'

'And I shouldn't have had to ride for help in such a hurry.'

'Go on,' I urged hopefully.

'Then I might never again have jumped anything bigger than that little breakwater.'

'So?' I dared to prompt.

'So if I ever get back into the show ring, it'll be thanks to you, Jackie. That's the truth.'

'You're a sport, Paul.' Warmly I said what I'd really always known at heart: 'A real hundred per cent *sport*.'

CHAPTER FIFTEEN

HAPPY PONY DAYS

Dear Mum and Dad,
I wrote quickly because the daylight was fading, and now only the sunset-glow lit up the inside of the tent.

Nobody will be able to ride Misty for the rest of the camp, but the vet says her leg should heal up all right. He's coming to see her every day.

Poor Misty! She does feel forsaken when the other ponies go out, because she enjoyed the rides and outings so much before she tore her leg. Still, she's getting a lot of extra fuss, and you know how she enjoys that, and she has got Daydream within whinnying distance in the same block of looseboxes. Most of the day she stands with her head over the door,

*watching whatever's going on, and calling
to everybody who goes past.*

  *But, just as important, I want to tell you
about Paul.*

I broke off my letter as I thought of Paul. The
old saying: 'To understand all is to forgive all,'
came to my mind. Yes, it was easy to forgive
Paul now that I knew *everything*.

Sheila had at last confided in Babs and
me. I suppose she knew that Paul would
no longer mind our knowing the whole truth.
First Sheila showed me a cutting from the local
newspaper, dated about two years ago. There
was a headline:

DAYDREAM WINS THE DAY FOR
SHOW-JUMPING TWINS

Underneath was a picture of Pete and Paul,
both looking happy and confident, standing on
either side of Daydream. Then there were
the words: '*Paul and Peter Wayne share the
six-year-old mare Daydream, taking it in turns
to enter her for different classes at local shows
and are starting to be successful. Both won a
cup apiece at the Fairfield Show last week.*'

123

That was the only cup that Paul won because, only three weeks later, he was riding Daydream in some Jumping Trials when the calamity happened. The riders were started in pairs, one a few minutes after the others. Paul had to follow a girl called Ann Adams. The jumps were quite big and the course was twisting, a real cross-country course.

Then Ann Adams fell off at a thick brush hedge, with a ditch on the far side. Her pony was down, too, but Paul didn't see them, and, by an unlucky fluke, the steward's attention was diverted by something else. There was no one to warn Paul. He took the jump and saw the girl lying half-out of the ditch on the far side.

Paul dragged at Daydream's reins, trying to turn her in midair. The mare fell. She rolled on Paul and broke his thigh. It was fractured in two places, and he was in hospital for weeks.

When Paul was off his crutches and ready to try to jump again, he would sit in his saddle as stiff as a toy soldier. His hands trembled on the reins. However, he made himself ride to the jump. Then he'd always pull Daydream aside, and say he just couldn't face it. Sheila and Pete tried to encourage him, but he kept on telling them not to fuss. Paul felt sure he would never jump again. His bitterness became intense. Soon the green-eyed monster, jealousy, reared its horrid head. When the summer came, the other twin, Pete, jumped from triumph to triumph, winning rosettes and cups at almost every show. I could imagine Paul feeling jealous and bitter.

In the end Sheila and Pete decided to put away the cups and rosettes. They never mentioned show-jumping in Paul's presence. It was the taboo subject. They'd decided that Paul must go at his own pace, and they hoped that, if no one made a fuss or badgered him, he might solve his problem in his own way and in his own time.

I picked up my pen again, and switched on my torch because the evening light had almost gone.

And that is what happened, thanks to Fate, and, in a way, to me. I went on writing to Mum and Dad. *Well, at the moment Paul is making haste slowly. He's realized that he isn't ready to jump Daydream yet. He's apt to snatch at her mouth, and of course he doesn't want to risk spoiling her chances for when Pete enters her for the Springfield Show. Paul's still jumping every day. He's practising on Bess who, as it turns out, is just the pony for the job. She's quiet and steady, so that Paul can knot the reins and just hang on to a neck-strap until he gets confidence.*

I think he knows he may never catch up with Pete in the show-jumping ring, and I suppose that's still disappointing for him, but I expect he'll be able to jump as well as most of us. The important thing seems to be that he's made himself overcome his fear and he doesn't feel a coward any more.

Just then I heard running footsteps over the grass outside. Babs's head appeared round the tent flap.

'Come on, Jackie,' my cousin urged. 'Finish your letter tomorrow. Guess who's sent me to find you – Paul.'

Yet another sing-song in the barn . . . I could already hear the wheeze of Pete's mouth-organ, Sheila's tinkle-tankle on the piano, and the twang of an off-tune guitar as we sped through the falling dusk.

Then the thump-thump of a drum was added to the so-called music. When we entered the barn I saw Paul behind a battered drum-set. He smiled across at us, did a thumbs-up sign, and performed a fanfare roll on the drum for our benefit.

'Cheers!' I said to Babs. 'Paul's actually glad to see us.'

A harvest moon shone through the open doorway of the barn, and a white owl flapped across the yard.

One song ended and another was begun. I smiled across at Babs. Yes, this would be something always to remember with happiness after all – our pony camp summer.

Jackie and the
Pony-Boys

Judith M. Berrisford

Hodder
Children's
Books

a division of Hodder Headline plc

Jackie and the Pony-Boys

Contents

CHAPTER ONE

GIRLS NOT WANTED

'Wake up, Jackie.'

I roused myself from pony dreams to find my cousin, Babs, shaking me while my golden cocker spaniel, Scamp, tugged at the bed-clothes.

'Come on,' Babs urged. 'Three boys with ponies are making jumps in the lower meadow. Let's wake Pam.'

We hurried to our friend's bedroom. (By the way, I ought to explain that we were staying with Pam, at her parents' farm, for the summer holidays.) Soon we were on Pam's bed telling her the intriguing news about the boys.

Then, a little later, the three of us – now clad in shirts and jeans – ran out of the farmhouse and clambered over the rails into the meadow just as the boys were riding their ponies over the jumps.

'Hi,' Babs called to the boys.

'Hullo,' a freckle-faced, sandy-haired boy said, and the other two reined up with slightly blank expressions.

'Carry on jumping,' Babs said in a friendly way. 'We're just going back to have a quick breakfast and then we'll get our ponies.'

The boys looked at each other dubiously and dismounted, and there was an awkward silence.

'Make some more jumps if you like,' Pam invited, to break the silence. 'Daddy won't mind as long as you don't pull the hedge down.'

'Then we'll join you,' I added. 'We need some jumping practice.'

'Hey, not so fast,' said the eldest boy at last. He crammed his riding hat farther down over his dark hair. 'Couldn't you girls go and jump somewhere else?'

'We could,' said Babs, hurt. 'But why should we? We've more right to be here than you have. This field belongs to Pam's father.'

The dark boy frowned. 'Does it?'

'Yes. You're in the wrong field.' Pam pointed to a curve of pollards along a winding stream. 'The willow brook marks the boundary.'

'I see,' said the freckle-faced boy, rubbing his pony's neck and looking disconcerted.

'Then we're the ones who'd better buzz off. We're trespassing.'

'Not really,' said Pam.

'And there's no hurry to go,' Babs added.

'I think there is,' the dark-haired boy said pointedly, and added to his companions: 'Come on, you two.'

We watched as the three boys gathered up their reins and put their feet into their near stirrup irons before swinging themselves into their saddles.

'See you,' Babs called hopefully as the boys turned their ponies towards the brook, and trotted away from us, a shaft of sunlight glinting on the metal of a new shoe on the hoof of the freckle-faced boy's chestnut pony.

'Hey, come back,' I called impulsively. 'We're sorry we barged in.'

'You're welcome to jump in our field,' shouted Pam. 'Daddy won't mind.'

The freckle-faced boy glanced back, and the other two drew ahead.

'Please jump here,' I shouted.

'No thanks,' the dark boy called to us – and to the third boy who was lagging, 'Buck up, Tim.'

I gave a heavy sigh as I turned to Babs and

Pam. 'They just don't want to be bothered with us.'

'Oh, forget about them,' said Pam. 'We can make our own fun.'

'Who do they think they are anyway?' demanded Babs when we went back to Holly Farm for breakfast.

'The dark-haired boy's Derek Emett; and the freckle-faced one's his cousin, Tim Green,' explained Pam. 'Tim's parents were killed in a car crash and so he lives with Derek's parents. The fair one's a second cousin of Derek's who's staying with them. I'm not sure of his name. None of them have lived in the district long. Derek's father's a doctor who took over the practice at Hilton Rise when old Doctor Brown had a stroke.'

'Tim seemed more friendly than the others,' I said; and then we tried to put the boys from our minds.

After breakfast we cantered our ponies along the green lane to Brocksby Heath. Then we climbed to the ridge, and halted for a breather while we looked towards the sand-fringed sea. We turned to ride home. Halfway back, Pam's pony, Strawberry, developed a loose shoe, so we had to make a detour and go round by the smithy at Little Dainton.

It was nearly lunch time when we rode back along the green lane to Holly Farm. Over the hedge we could see the jumps that the boys had now made in Mr Marlow's field – five fences of brushwood and gorse, rather wide and of varying heights. There was no sign of the boys. I expect they'd gone to lunch.

We reined up and gazed at the course, tempted to try our ponies.

'Now's our chance,' decided Babs.

'Here goes,' said Pam, riding Strawberry up to the gate, and bending over the pony's withers to lift the catch.

We rode into the field, and, one after the other, set our ponies at the jumps. Patch, with Babs in the saddle, shook his head and fought all the way to the first fence.

I rode past them. 'I'll give you a lead, Babs,' I offered. My pony, Misty, was ready for anything. She cantered to the first obstacle, timing it just right, took off and cleared it neatly, cantering on to the next one. Behind us came Strawberry and Pam.

Suddenly Patch decided that he did not want to be left behind. He hurled himself forward just as Strawberry was coming to the second jump. Together they approached the take-off.

'Keep back, Babs,' warned Pam.

Babs wrenched at Patch's head. Obstinately the skewbald pony kept on his collision course.

Too late Pam tried to turn Strawberry away from the jump. The roan checked. Patch cannoned into her, throwing her off her balance. Together the two ponies crashed into the jump. Pam was flung head-over-heels as Strawberry pitched forward. Patch came down, too, and Babs only just managed to kick her feet out of the stirrups before her pony rolled.

Babs disappeared among a flurry of threshing hooves and heaving pony bodies. Aghast, I jumped down to help.

'Stand clear,' sternly called a boy's voice.

Led by the dark-haired Derek Emett, the three boys burst on to the scene of disaster.

While Tim jumped to the ground to help, the fair-haired boy held his pony's reins.

Pam was dazedly getting to her feet. Tim and Derek grabbed Babs by the shoulders and pulled her clear of the struggling ponies. Patch was the first pony to regain his feet. With broken reins trailing, he stood shaking his head and snorting, while Strawberry, saddle awry, heaved himself up.

'Th-thanks for saving us,' Babs faltered.

'You silly girls,' scolded Derek. 'Now you

know why we didn't want you to get in the way.'

'You and your ponies might have been hurt,' added Tim, looking concerned.

'Girls!' exclaimed the fair-haired boy. 'Trust you to cause chaos. It took us half an hour to make that jump.'

'Well, we'll build it up again for you,' Babs offered, rushing to drag some of the brushwood back into place.

'No, thank you,' Derek said firmly. 'If you want to make amends just keep right out of our way. Understand?'

'Message received.' I sighed as we pulled the reins over our ponies' heads, and trooped, defeated, to the field gate. 'We know when we're not wanted.'

CHAPTER TWO

BUT DOES TIM NEED US?

That afternoon Pam's father decided to carry the hay from Seven Acres, the big field on top of the hill. Rain had been forecast for the next day and Mr Wells was anxious to get the hay under cover before nightfall.

So everybody on the farm was needed to give a hand. Babs, Pam and I were raking the ripened hay into small haycocks while Mr Wells drove the tractor pulling the big hay float, and Pam's mother forked up the loads.

Scamp was delighted with the haymaking. He chased mice – real and imaginary – and snuffled happily into the haycocks. He was getting in everybody's way, but nobody seemed to mind. It was fun, loading the hay in the sunshine. Though the grass stalks were scratchy to our legs and arms, and towards the evening the midges started to bite, we were all enjoying ourselves.

Scamp came and lay beside us, pink tongue lolling, while we sat under a shady oak for our break. We drank cold tea from lemonade bottles and munched crusty slices of bread with cheese and farm butter, and Pam's mother's special home-made fruit cake.

'Back to work, everybody,' Mr Wells decided all too soon. 'Not long now and we'll have finished.'

Babs and I tried not to groan. Our backs and arms were beginning to ache and it was difficult to get back into the rhythm of the haymaking. To make things worse we could see the three boys trotting along the lane on their way back from a ride. We felt left out. The boys had made it only too clear that they didn't want us, and Derek had been downright unpleasant.

Boys versus girls. Was that how it was going to be? Or were the boys going to ignore us during the rest of the pony holiday?

I felt hurt and angry. It wasn't fair. Why couldn't the boys give us a chance?

Pony-boys! I wielded my hayfork furiously. We just couldn't forget those boys – not when they were so near for so much of the time, practising jumping in the field beyond the brook.

'For goodness' sake stop fuming about the boys,' said Babs, reading my thoughts. 'They're not worth it.'

'I know,' I groaned, 'but I can't help wondering what they're doing now. They stopped jumping and rode off over an hour ago.'

'Another three loads and we'll have finished,' called Pam's father from the wagon. 'You girls are doing well.'

We went on loading, and then I stopped as I saw my spaniel Scamp, who had been snoozing against a rick, suddenly come to life and streak after a bolting rabbit.

'Oh dear!' I dropped the hayfork and ran to follow Scamp. If I didn't get him back he would chase that rabbit and then just follow his nose until he was miles away.

I scrambled over the fence, into the wood, and ran through the ferns and brambles of the undergrowth in the direction of Scamp's excited yelps.

'Scamp!' I kept shouting. 'Come back, you silly dog.'

Not taking any notice of me, Scamp snuffled after the scent, nose to the ground, questing this way and that, and all the time getting deeper into the wood.

'Scamp, where are you?' I panted, and then

leaned against a sycamore to get enough breath to whistle.

'Hey, there!' A boy's voice shouted from another part of the wood. 'I've got your dog.'

'I'm on my way,' I called, following a stream through a clump of hollies, clambering over a tumbledown wall, squelching across a boggy patch, and stumbling over some tree roots.

Scamp barked as he heard me.

'Here we are,' the boy called and I rounded a thicket to see Scamp wriggling in the arms of a sandy-haired, freckle-faced boy who was sitting on a fallen tree – Tim.

'Hullo,' Tim greeted me. 'I wondered whether he was your dog.'

I smiled, relieved to have my hopes confirmed – that one of the pony-boys wanted to be friendly.

Meanwhile Scamp, tail a-wag, darted a quick look at me as though to say: 'Look what a good friend I've made,' and twisted his head round to give the boy's chin a dab with his tongue.

I sat down on the tree trunk beside the boy and ruffled Scamp's neck.

'He's taken a liking to you, Tim,' I said.

'He's a super dog,' Tim said, and added quietly, 'just like my Goldie.'

'Have you got a spaniel, too?' I asked, and then noticed a sad look in the boy's eyes.

'I used to have.' The boy put his cheek against Scamp's head and his voice was muffled. 'He was very like Scamp – the same floppy ears and big feet. I expect he'll be about the same age now.'

'Scamp's four,' I told him?

'Well, Goldie would be about five,' said Tim.

'Where is he now?' I asked. 'Did you have to sell him?'

'Sell him?' Tim echoed. 'I'd never have sold him. I lost him.'

'Lost him!' My hand trembled on Scamp's ruffled front, and I thought how dreadful I'd feel if I ever lost him. 'What happened?'

Tim looked away. 'There was an accident.' I'll never forget the dead tone of his voice as he said that. 'Mum and Dad were . . .' He broke off. 'That was the worst of it. Goldie was with them in the car, when it happened.'

I didn't know what to say. I could imagine what it would have been like if anything had happened to my mother and father – and if Scamp had been lost as well . . .

Tim's hand tightened on Scamp's shoulder so that my spaniel looked up at him, puzzled.

'There was no trace of Goldie after the crash. He must have run away. Perhaps he was dazed. Of course, he might have crawled off to die, but we never found him. My uncle and Derek and I searched everywhere and we made inquiries.'

I stroked Scamp's head. 'I'm so sorry,' was all I could say.

'I expect Goldie's dead.' Tim sighed. 'I've got to accept the fact that I'll never see him again. He was probably injured and just crawled in a ditch to die.'

Just then I heard Babs and Pam calling me.

'Jackie, where are you?'

At the sound of their voices, Tim got up from the tree trunk, and Scamp looked up appealingly as though to say: 'Don't go.'

'I'll be off,' said Tim. 'Derek and Giles will be wondering where I am.'

I nodded. I could guess his feelings. Sometimes he must like to go off by himself, perhaps to think about the old days. I knew how he felt at this moment. He did not want Babs's and Pam's questions, and a lot of fuss.

'*Jackie!*'

'Coming,' I shouted in the direction of Babs's voice. 'Well, I expect I'll be seeing you again,' I said to Tim. 'I suppose you'll be practising jumping with your friends in Mr Marlow's field.'

'Yes,' said Tim. 'We'll be there most days. Sorry we had to choke you off, but we're putting in some serious practice. Derek's keen on our entering for the team-jumping at Oakworth.'

There was a rush of footsteps on mossy ground, and the cracking of twigs as Babs and Pam approached.

Tim gave Scamp's ears a last fondle. 'Look after yourself, beauty,' he said to my spaniel. 'Be seeing you.' Then he dodged out of sight among the trees and was gone, while Scamp gazed after him, as though to say: 'I've made a new friend.'

Yes, I thought – and so perhaps have I. That is if only the two horrid boys, Derek and Giles, will let us be friends.

I sighed. It didn't seem likely. The boys, even Tim, might believe that girls spelt at the worst 'trouble' and at the best 'nuisance'.

CHAPTER THREE

FATE TAKES A HAND

During the next few days I kept thinking about Tim. It must be dreadful for him to have lost his mother and father and dog so suddenly, and, with such a grumpy and difficult cousin as Derek, it could not be pleasant for him living with the Emetts.

He was missing his parents, and his dog, Goldie, terribly. That was easy to see. It was impossible, of course, to bring back his mother and father and it was almost certain that Goldie was dead, too, but there was still Scamp. Tim had taken such a liking to my dog, and Scamp was so like his own Goldie, that I wondered whether my spaniel might not, in some way, be able to ease the pain of Tim's great loss.

I kept thinking along these lines from the moment I woke up in the morning until restlessly I fell asleep at night. Whether I was helping Babs and Pam – with Scamp's hindrance – to bring in the cows for milking, or to take them back to their field, or feeding the chickens and ducks, and shutting them up for the night, safe from the fox, I felt sick at heart, being so sorry for Tim, and yet so unable to help.

Even when we were out riding, my mind turned from Misty and the good times we were having in the summery countryside to the lonely and heartbroken boy.

I had told Babs and Pam that the boys were practising for the team-jumping at Oakworth, and from our bedroom window we could see them, on their ponies, three abreast, training over the jumps which they had made in Marlow's field. We decided to have a go at team-jumping ourselves, and we made some jumps in Seven Acres. We thought we had better keep right away from the boys' practice area so that they would not see us, and think that we were hanging around them.

All the same we kept catching glimpses of them, and I could not help noticing that, although Tim was cheerful and quite lively when he was talking and joking with Derek and Giles, whenever there were quiet moments his face took on a sad, hopeless expression.

One day, I saw Tim looking like that. He was standing by his pony, tightening his girths while Derek and Giles were rebuilding a jump which they had knocked down. Suddenly, Tim brushed his sleeve across his eyes. Then he seemed to take a grip on himself. He squared his shoulders, and swinging himself into the saddle, galloped round the field. Then, with an effort, he set his pony at the jumps. He cleared the first three, but then crashed down the fence that Derek and Giles had just built up.

'Tim, you clot!' Derek shouted crossly. 'What do you think you're doing?'

'Yes, why didn't you wait until we could all jump together?' demanded fair-haired Giles. 'We've just made up that jump, and now you've knocked it all down again.'

'Oh, shut up.' Tim sounded irritable, not at all the way he'd been the other day with Scamp and me.

He jumped down from his pony and stooped to pick up the scattered branches and brushwood. From where I was watching I could see, from the droop of his shoulders, that he was utterly downhearted.

Suddenly my mind was made up. I knew what I would do, and I wasn't going to tell Babs and Pam my plan in case they tried to stop me.

Making an excuse that I wanted to give Scamp a run before lunch I dashed up to the bedroom to change my shoes. Scamp followed me up the stairs, and dabbed at my hand with his cold nose as I sat down at the dressing table, and picking up my Biro, began hastily to dash off a note:

Dear Tim,

Scamp took such a liking to you when we met in the woods, and – since it's a bit difficult giving him enough exercise here on the farm because he wants to play with all the animals and chase the hens – I wondered whether you could take him out now and then. It would be a help, and I know Scamp would love it –

'Jackie!' The back door slammed and I could hear Babs and Pam running into the hall below.

'Coming,' I called and hoped that they wouldn't dash upstairs to the bedroom. 'I won't be a moment.'

I wrote quickly:

If this doesn't seem to be a good idea, don't bother to reply. I'll understand.

Then I signed the letter: *Your friend (I hope!), Jackie.*

I didn't have a chance after all to deliver the note that day. So, as soon as breakfast was over next morning, I whistled Scamp and told Babs and Pam that I would join them for some jumping practice of our own later. Then I set off for Hilton Rise where Tim lived.

It was a lovely morning, and I'd never seen Scamp so full of life. He bounded ahead, snuffing at the grass for scents, and chasing imaginary rabbits, and every now and then stopping to look back at me just to make sure that I was still following him.

He paused to watch inquisitively a white butterfly that had alighted on a harebell. Then he stalked it, comically flattening himself, and, with paw raised exaggeratedly high, stretched his neck forward to sniff at it. The butterfly, gossamer-winged, tickled Scamp's nose as it fluttered to another blossom. With a joyful bark Scamp leapt high into the air in hopeless, but happy, pursuit.

We crossed the common and I called Scamp to heel as we entered the village of Hilton Rise. Dr Emett's house was at the end of the cluster of grey stone cottages with sunny gardens. It stood a little way back from the road at the end of a gravel drive. With Scamp at my side, I went through the open gateway, and rounded a clump of rhododendrons to reach the front door.

I'd just pushed my letter through the letter-box and was about to go away when there came a clatter of hooves from the lane and, over the hedge, I could see the heads and shoulders of the three pony-boys as they came back from an early ride.

Scamp heard the hooves, and smelt ponies. I suppose he thought they were Strawberry, Patch and Misty, with Babs and Pam coming to meet us. Before I could grasp his collar and hold him, he darted out of the drive towards the ponies, barking a welcome.

I heard Derek shout: 'Look out!' followed by a pony snort.

'Hey, watch it!' warned Tim amid a shuffle of sidestepping hooves.

'Scamp, come here,' I called, running out of the drive to see my dog, ears flattened, tail tucked down, trapped in the middle of a pother of startled ponies.

Giles's pony – a showy bay – lowered his head to sniff Scamp inquiringly. At the same time Tim's pony brushed him with his foreleg, as Tim jumped down in an attempt to lift Scamp out of harm's way, but the touch of the pony's leg was enough to frighten Scamp. With a terrified bark he ran at Derek's tall chestnut, and nipped the back tendon of his near hind leg. The chestnut squealed, and lashed out. His hoof caught Scamp on the head, and, yelping, my spaniel spun round, and then lay still on the dusty road.

'Oh, Scamp,' I gasped in horror. 'What's happened to you?'

Tim was on his knees beside Scamp. We looked at the unconscious form. Scamp's fore-leg twitched; then he was still again. There was no wound on his head, just the imprint of part of the chestnut's shoe flattened on his silky skull.

'He's breathing,' said Tim.

'But only just,' I said tearfully.

With an effort I pulled myself together.

It was obvious that Scamp was badly hurt, and I knew that a blow on the head was dangerous. What ought we to do?

Derek and Giles tied up their ponies and came, soberly, towards us.

'Why can't you control your dog?' Derek demanded. 'I hadn't a chance. Your dog just ran among us.'

'I know.' I nodded miserably. 'I ought to have had him on a lead.'

Then Tim, with wonderful gentleness, carried Scamp indoors and into the kitchen.

Meanwhile Derek telephoned the vet from the hall. He came back with my unopened note to Tim in his hand, then went out again.

'For you, Tim,' he said.

Tim read the note, passed a hand over his forehead, and looked from Scamp's still body to me, and touched my arm.

'Oh, Jackie,' he sighed. 'Why do you do these things?'

'Good intentions,' I said ruefully. 'I thought if you had a sort of share in Scamp, it would make up for your losing Goldie – both dogs being golden cockers, you see.'

'Tim!' came an imperative shout from Derek. 'For heaven's sake stop nattering to that goofy girl and give us a hand with the ponies. They're eating Dad's delphiniums.'

'More trouble,' said Tim. 'Now Derek will be more convinced than ever that girls are bad luck to us.'

CHAPTER FOUR

TOUCH AND GO

'Severe concussion,' said Mr Windall, the vet, after a thorough examination of Scamp.

'Is that bad?' asked Tim, voicing my thoughts.

'Well, it means that Scamp will need careful nursing,' the vet said. 'We must keep him warm and quiet.' He crossed to the kitchen window, and partly drew the curtains. 'We don't want too much light in here.'

'Oh, dear, can't I take him home?' I asked.

'Moving him is quite out of the question,' said Mr Windall. He took a syringe from his case, and held it to the light while he expelled any air bubbles. 'I'm going to give Scamp a shot. After that, I want you to fill a hot water bottle – not too hot, mind – and put it against his tummy, to counteract the shock. Understand?'

I looked helplessly at Tim. He was the one who would have to cope.

'I'll see to everything,' he decided. 'Scamp won't be disturbed. He'll stay right here, in the kitchen, until it's safe for him to be moved. Don't worry, Jackie.'

'Thanks, Tim.'

Then the vet left, and a moment later the other boys came into the kitchen. My heart thumped as Giles picked up my note which Tim had dropped on the table. He made an exasperated sound as he read it. He passed the note to Derek.

'So this is how it all came about,' groaned Derek, turning to me. 'You girls barging in again. My first instinct was right. Trouble follows you wherever you go. You're bad luck – jinxed.' Then he must have noticed how forlorn I looked, because he turned away and said over his shoulder, as he went to find a hot water bottle for Tim to fill, 'Well, it's not Scamp's fault, having such a zany owner as you. So we'll see this thing through. But afterwards, don't take advantage of us and get the idea that you can hang around. Understand?'

Dr Emett's house was a busy place, what with the two doctors coming in from their rounds,

Mrs Emett busy with her committees, and Miss Griffiths, the receptionist, taking telephone messages, answering the doorbell, and filling in forms.

Nevertheless my spaniel and I, for the next few hours, seemed to be the hub of that hectic household.

Both doctors came in to look at Scamp, and to raise his eyelids to assess his condition, and Nurse Griffiths refilled the hot water bottle.

I didn't leave Scamp's side. So Tim telephoned Holly Farm to let the others know what had happened, and to deter Babs and Pam from coming over and inflicting still more pony-girls on the Emett household.

Mrs Emett asked me to wash up the lunch dishes, because she was rushing to preside at a Women's Institute meeting. Dr Emett had an afternoon surgery, and his partner went out on his rounds while the three boys rode off to Marlow's field for more jumping practice.

So there I was – in the Emetts' kitchen – quite alone with my unconscious spaniel.

An hour ticked by. Then suddenly Scamp's nose gave a slight twitch. I held my breath as I saw his eyelids flicker. His eyes opened. They had a glazed and faraway look. Was he coming round?

'Scamp!' I whispered urgently. 'Can you hear me, Scamp?'

Was it my imagination or did his stubby tail give a feeble thump?

Scamp tried to raise his head. The effort was too much. He gave a throaty grunt and lay very still.

Was he dying? Or even already dead?

'Don't go, Scamp – *don't*.'

My plea ended in sobs. I went down on my knees to press my head against his seemingly lifeless body. I held my breath to listen for his heartbeat. Thank goodness! There it was – slow, but fairly strong and quite steady.

'Stay with me, Scamp – stay!'

Was Scamp going to live after all? In a surge of relief, I found that I could not hold back my feelings. Thinking I was quite alone I wept so loudly that I did not hear hooves on the gravel outside or footsteps on the tiles.

Then I saw a shadow and looked up, ashamed.

Through my tears I saw Tim looking down at me.

'We ought not to have left you alone, Jackie,' he said. 'That's why I've come back. How is Scamp? What's happened?'

I told him how Scamp had seemed to come

round and then fall into such deep unconsciousness that I thought he had died.

'Gosh, Jackie! No wonder you were upset.' He brought up a chair and sat beside me. 'I'll take over for a spell. The others will be back soon. You could start getting tea, if you'd like to make yourself useful.'

I put on the kettle, and set out the tea cups on the trolley, ready to push through to the sitting room when everybody came home. I cut some bread and butter and made it as thin as I could. I wanted to do something to show Dr and Mrs Emett how grateful I was for their kindness in letting me stay to keep an eye on Scamp. It was bad enough for them to have a sick dog in the kitchen without a strange girl inflicted on them, as well. I took some cake from a tin on one of the shelves, and put it on a plate. I was just spooning out some strawberry jam in the pantry when Tim's voice almost made me drop the dish.

'Jackie! Quickly. I think he's coming round.'

I dashed into the kitchen, and knelt beside Scamp. His eyes were wide open now, and he was looking at Tim as if he were trying to focus on him. Was he trying to remember where he had seen this boy before? Or could he not quite see whether anyone was there at all?

'Scamp.' I put out my hand gently to stroke his golden head. 'I'm here, Scamp. You put up a gallant fight and you've won.'

'That's right, my beauty,' Tim said softly. 'You're going to get well now.'

Scamp tried to raise his head. He gave a tiny wuffle. 'There, there,' I soothed, holding him. 'Don't try to move.'

As though he recognized my voice, Scamp's pink tongue came out and he gave a limp dab at my hand.

Tim turned to me. 'There's one thing we ought to settle before the others come back, Jackie,' he told me.

'Scamp won't be able to be moved from here tonight, and you can't very well stay up all night with him here all by yourself.'

'I wouldn't mind,' I said.

'I know.' He looked straight at me. 'But that's not the point. The others might raise objections. You've got to trust me with Scamp, Jackie. I'll sit up with him. I'll watch over him, take just as much care of him as if he were my own Goldie.'

'I know you will, Tim.' I smiled my gratitude. 'I'll never be able to forget this.'

'I hope you will,' he said, turning away.

'Will what?' I echoed.

'Forget it,' he said. 'Forget that Derek and his dad let Scamp stay here, for instance?'

I sighed.

'So you agree with what Derek said – that you don't want us girls to be under any obligation? You want to be rid of us as well?'

He didn't say anything.

'That's it, isn't it, Tim?' I walked to the window. 'Oh you don't have to answer. I know it.'

'No, it isn't like that,' Tim blurted out. 'That's how it is with Derek and Giles – but not with me. I wouldn't mind having you and Babs and Pam as friends. But what can I do? I'm living here as a sort of guest. I haven't got a home of my own. Derek's landed with me. I've got to play along with him, do what he wants.'

'Yes, I see that –' I broke off as I heard the clatter of hooves on the gravel. 'They're back. You'd better make yourself scarce. Derek will be mad if he sees you're with me. I'll look after Scamp until I go home.'

'I'll stay,' Tim groaned uneasily. 'But watch it with Derek. Please – watch it!'

CHAPTER FIVE

SOMEBODY ELSE'S PONY

Derek was a difficult boy. That fact affected all of us. Giles followed his lead, and Tim had to do the same up to a point, because he'd made his home with Derek's mother and father.

Well, if Tim could put up with Derek, then surely I could.

I'd do what Tim advised: keep out of Derek's way. If ever I did have to be in his company, I'd watch myself – that I didn't arouse his jealousy or insecurity, or any of the other instincts that made Derek such a grumpy boy.

I thought how different things might be if only Tim had been my cousin. Mummy and Daddy could have given him a home, and Babs and I could have treated him like one of the family and shared his pony interests.

If wishes were horses, beggars would ride! I told myself that I must come down to earth, and to face life as it was and not daydream of might-have-beens.

I switched all my thoughts to Scamp, willing him to get better, and, sure enough, after two nights at the Emetts' he was well enough to be brought home.

Although still shaky, Scamp padded round the living room at the farmhouse, sniffing, and then, with an effort, heaved himself up into his favourite chair, turned round on the cushion and settled down to doze.

After lunch Babs and Pam took Misty, Patch and Strawberry to the smithy. Strawberry's shoe had again worked loose. As Misty and Patch were also due to be shod, we decided it would be better for them all to go to Little Dainton together. So, as Mrs Wells had gone shopping, and Mr Wells was busy in the fields, Scamp and I were left alone. We were not on our own for long, however, because presently Tim rode up to see how Scamp was progressing. I was surprised and delighted. Perhaps Tim had decided not to let his life be ruled by Derek after all.

'It's good to see you, Tim,' I greeted him. 'Now Scamp will know he's not forsaken by his old friends.'

Tim sat down, and gently picked up my

spaniel to nurse him. 'That's right – sleep back to health, my beauty.'

'If you could stay and dog-watch for a while, Tim,' I said, 'I'll borrow Pam's bike and ride over to the vet's for Scamp's new tablets.'

However, Pam's bike had a flat tyre, and when I tried to pump it up I found that the valve rubber had perished.

I went back to the living room, intending to ask Tim whether he would ride over for the tablets as his pony, Robin, was here. But Scamp looked so contented with his head nestled into the crook of Tim's arm, and his golden body sprawled on the boy's lap, that I hadn't the heart to disturb him.

'Oh, Tim,' I began. 'Pam's bike is out of action, and Scamp does need the tablets. He's due for a couple at four o'clock. I had intended to ask you to take Robin and fetch them, but Scamp's so well settled, and having such a good sleep, that I think it would be better not to disturb him.'

Tim looked fondly down at Scamp's sleeping head. 'I don't mind sitting here for an hour or so, and letting him snooze.'

'Yes, and it's doing him the world of good. But we've got to have the tablets, so would you mind, Tim, if I borrow Robin to fetch them?'

Tim seemed to be considering the matter. Then he looked again at Scamp. 'I suppose it would be all right,' he said reluctantly, 'if you're sure you can manage him?'

'Goodness, yes,' I said confidently. 'I've had a pony of my own for years, and ridden all sorts of other ponies. Besides I've sometimes helped in riding stables and pony camps. I'm thoroughly pony-wise.'

'Very well,' said Tim though he still sounded doubtful. 'I suppose this is a bit of an emergency, and Robin is an easy pony to ride.'

'Thanks, Tim,' I said, hurrying off before he could change his mind. I was looking forward to trying out Tim's pony. I'd seen him jumping and he looked a wonderful ride. Hurrying to the stables, I spoke cheerily to Robin, patted him, and pulled up his girths. Then, shortening the stirrup leathers a hole, I led him out of the yard, gathered up the reins, and swung myself into the saddle.

Robin moved off briskly, glad to be on the move. We trotted down the lane and then, sensing his wish for a canter, I turned him on to the roadside verge.

Tim's pony was just as good a ride as he looked. He swung along with smooth strides, sensitive to the lightest touch on the reins or to the leg aids. A gully led from the road to the ditch, and Robin cleared it easily with barely a squeeze from my legs.

We reached the cross-roads and I pulled him up, hesitating. Should we go along the main road to the vet's, or should we turn up the green lane, and ride across the common?

The way over the common was slightly longer, but, in spite of that, I knew that if we took that route we would get there sooner because we could canter most of the way.

Robin's ears were pricked as he looked towards the green lane. He tossed his head and pulled at the reins. There was no doubt at all as to which way he wanted to go.

'Very well, Robin.' I patted his neck and rode him carefully over the cross-roads to the green lane. 'You want a good pipe-opener, and so do I. So we may as well both enjoy ourselves.' I raised myself in my stirrups and shortened the reins. 'Come on. Let's go.'

Robin broke into an eager canter. The hedges sped past as he pounded over the soft turf. Neck extended and mane flying, he began to gallop as we reached the hill that led to the common. This was super. Tim's pony was an even better ride than my own beloved Misty. I suppose it was because Robin was bigger, and maybe I was getting just a bit tall for Misty. It was great to feel his powerful stride and his eagerness to respond to my mood.

We reached the common and I set him to jump over a fallen tree trunk just for the sheer joy of living. Robin cleared it like a bird, and cantered on. High overhead a lark was singing, and my heart sang, too. It was a lovely day. Scamp was going to get better, and Tim seemed happier for having a share in him. Robin was a wonderful pony, and we were having a fabulous time. Everything in the world seemed right. I suppose that ought to have warned me because, in this life, just when everything seems to be perfect, and there isn't a cloud in the sky, so to speak, that is just when something dreadful happens. Disaster always lies just round the corner, waiting for the unwary – for that over-optimistic moment that leads to one doing something rash.

I suppose I was being rash in taking advantage of Tim's good-natured permission to ride Robin, and in giving him such a hectic cross-country gallop, but I didn't think of that.

Robin was such an easy ride and I was feeling so happy that it seemed as though nothing could go wrong. I sped on – jinxed as usual!

We cantered to the top of the rise towards

41

some windswept birches and a solitary pine. I pulled up Robin for a breather. Then, thinking it was time we got the tablets and headed back to Tim and Scamp, I turned Robin towards the village, leaving the sandy track only to take a couple of gorse jumps that someone had made on the level ground near the brook.

Robin took these so easily that I was tempted to let him jump the stream. It wasn't very wide, and there seemed to be firm banks on both sides.

'Now for it, Robin.' I showed him the water. Then I turned him, rode him back a little way, wheeled him round, and set him at the jump at a canter.

Robin approached the brook eagerly, gathering himself for the take-off. Then, just as he was tensing himself ready to spring, the ground crumbled beneath him.

Robin threshed in the shallow water while I struggled to get off his neck. I slid, and landed knee-deep in the stream. Then, trying to keep clear in case he should roll, I grabbed Robin's head and urged him to his feet. He stood up, shaking himself, and then let me lead him, stumbling, through the stream and up the far bank. He was going short, limping badly. I stooped to examine his near fore, and groaned when I saw the bruised cut on his heel – an over-reach!

The shoe of Robin's near hind had caught the back of his foreleg when the bank had given way, cutting quite deeply into the flesh. Robin was badly lamed, and it was all my fault.

Why had I been so reckless? Why hadn't I just ridden straight to the vet's, keeping to the road, and not gone cantering and jumping over the common? Whatever would Tim think? That I wasn't to be trusted with somebody else's pony! And the dreadful thing was that he would be right. I couldn't imagine what had possessed me.

I wasn't worthy of Tim's friendship. Now he could only wish that he'd listened to Derek's warning and steered clear of all pony-girls!

CHAPTER SIX

MY SHAME

What a fool I'd been! Wet, miserable, and ashamed, I squeezed the stream water from my jeans, and running Robin's irons up the leathers, I pulled his reins over his head, and led him, limping badly, to the vet's.

'My husband's on his rounds,' Mrs Windall told me. Then noticing how wet and distraught I was, she asked, 'Can I help?'

'I hope so,' I said fervently. 'Please hurry.'

'I used to have ponies of my own,' she volunteered, following me. 'In fact I did quite a bit of jumping when I was your age so I do feel qualified to apply first-aid.' She bent to examine Robin's heel. 'It's a nasty over-reach. Bring him into the yard and I'll do my best to clean it up for you.'

Robin stood patiently while Mrs Windall

bathed his heel with salt and water. He was feeling sorry for himself and hung his head. The iodine that the vet's wife applied must have made the cut sting but beyond twitching his ears he made no protest.

'That should stop it getting infected,' Mrs Windall said, straightening up and patting Robin's neck. 'Of course, the bone may be bruised, so tell Tim to rest him for a day or two and if it gets puffy to apply hot fomentations.' My heart sank as she went on. 'This sort of injury can be very nasty. I've known it to put a pony out of action for weeks.'

I felt terrible as I led Robin, limping, homewards.

Tim and the other boys had been jumping so well together as a team, and had put in such hard work ready to enter the competition at Oakworth. Then I had to spoil everything for them; and now Derek and Giles would blame Tim for lending Robin to me.

'Jackie!'

I turned suddenly to see the vet's wife running after me. 'Tim Green has just rung up,' she told me breathlessly. 'You'd been away such a long time that he was afraid you'd had an accident. Anyway, I told him what had happened.'

45

'Oh, what did he say?'

'Well, he doesn't want you to take Robin back to the farm. He says that you're to leave him with me, and he'll come for him.'

'It's quite all right, Mrs Windall,' I began. 'It's no trouble. I don't mind taking Robin back – or perhaps Tim would rather I took him to the Emetts. I can easily do that.'

'No, Jackie,' Mrs Windall said firmly. 'I think Tim doesn't want to run a risk of anything else going wrong. He said quite definitely that you were to leave Robin with me, and get back to Scamp as quickly as possible.' She put out her hand to take Robin's bridle as a bus rattled into sight. 'You'd better catch the bus. Hurry up.'

So Tim didn't even trust me to lead his pony home. I suppose he'd never trust me again.

Just as I got off the bus at the end of the lane below Holly Farm I saw Tim jog-trotting into the main road on his way to collect Robin. I waved shamefacedly through the window, but he did not even see me. His freckled face looked flushed and strained as, hot and breathless, he hurried on. The bus stopped outside Holly Farm, and, dejected, I climbed down, crossed the road, and entered the farmyard.

'Is that you, Jackie?' came Babs's voice

from the living room window. 'Scamp's getting restless again. Have you got his tablets?'

My spaniel whined his pleasure at seeing me, and padded shakily across the room to sniff inquisitively at my damp jeans. 'Where have you been?' he seemed to say. 'What do you mean by going off and leaving me when I've been so poorly?'

I felt his nose. It was cold and damp, and his eyes looked clearer. There was no doubt that Scamp was on the mend. I gave him two of his tablets, lifted him up, and plumped him firmly back into his chair.

'Thank goodness,' said Babs. 'Now perhaps we can have some peace. Scamp's done nothing but whine and bark ever since Tim left him.'

'How – how was Tim?' I faltered.

'In quite a state. He told me to sit here with Scamp until you came back. Then he dashed off.'

'Was he very angry?'

'Angry? He might have been,' said Babs. 'Certainly he was worried about Robin. Can you blame him? It's no joke to have a pony lamed.'

'Babs!' Pam called from a little way off. 'Come and give me a hand in the tack room.'

47

A cloud came over the sun. The house seemed empty. I gazed forlornly out of the window, and Scamp looked up at me sensing my mood. Then he went to sleep and I was alone with my shame.

How could I face Tim again?

I felt even more guilty when, next morning, Babs and Pam coaxed me to join them in some jumping practice.

As we trotted and cantered right-handed and left-handed circles, and then figures of eight, we could hear the boys in Mr Marlow's meadow, hidden by a screen of trees.

'Come on, boy,' we heard Derek encouraging. 'Up!'

'Over!' added Giles.

Three boys – and two ponies ... The absence of Robin must be ruining their jumping practice. I couldn't give my mind to the schooling of Misty, and when the others suggested making a series of low jumps to form a jumping grid, my heart was not really in it. We completed the grid and rode our ponies up and down it several times, jumping them in and out over the low brushwood obstacles. Patch as usual was lazy and kept stopping and trying to run out, so Babs soon got bored.

'I'll leave you two to carry on,' she announced after a while. 'I'm going down to the village to see if Mr Trevelyan has finished repairing Patch's reins.'

Pam and I rode Misty and Strawberry over the grid again, and in spite of myself my spirits lightened. Misty was really good at this. She had become a nicely supple and well-balanced pony.

'Misty and Strawberry are both doing well,' I said to Pam as we halted for a breather. 'Let's try some pair-jumping for a change.'

We rode our ponies towards the circle of higher obstacles that Pam's father had built for us, and that always stood ready in the home field. There was a triple bar, consisting of three rows of poles on oil drums of varying heights, a post-and-rails, parallel bars and an in-and-out.

Side by side Pam and I cantered towards the post-and-rails. Stride for stride the ponies approached them, took off almost together, landed safely and set off for the next jump. Apart from Strawberry knocking down the top rail of the triple with her off-hind, we had a clear round. Well pleased with ourselves we patted our ponies, and made much of them before dismounting to replace the bars and deciding to make another obstacle with an old door that we dragged from the farmyard, and propped slanting on two bales of straw to encourage the ponies to spread themselves.

This time we didn't do quite so well. Misty did not like the look of the door, and she spoilt the round by refusing. Determined not to be beaten, I let her sniff the jump, and rode her at it again. She cleared it.

Pam and I were so absorbed in our jumping that it was some moments before we noticed Babs, in faded jeans and a check shirt, walking up the lane to the farmyard – minus her pony.

'Where's Patch?' I asked her.

'I've lent him to Tim,' announced Babs, with a bright smile. 'It was the only thing to do. Someone had to try to make amends for your blunder.'

I reeled in surprise and indignation.

'Why on earth didn't you tell us what you were going to do?' I demanded.

'I thought you'd try to stop me,' Babs said defiantly.

'But what did Tim say?' I asked.

'I didn't give him the chance to say anything,' said Babs. 'I just rode Patch straight to the Emetts' house. I knew the boys weren't there, because they were still jumping.'

'Then what did you do?' asked Pam.

'I unsaddled Patch and put him into one of their loose boxes,' said Babs. 'I left the saddle on the fence, and wrote a note and tucked it under the flap. I tore a page out of my Pony-Lovers' Diary, and wrote a message.'

'What did you write?' I asked, agog.

'I just said: "I hope Robin will soon be better. Meanwhile I'm lending you Patch. You'll be doing me a favour if you give him some jumping practice. And I'll be able to share Jackie's and Pam's ponies whenever I want a ride myself. So please accept the loan of Patch."'

I blinked. I'd known Babs all my life, but – from time to time – she still had the power to amaze me. She'd meant this kindly but, oh dear, what would Tim think now? That I'd been too mean-spirited to offer him Misty!

Suddenly I felt very annoyed with Babs.

'You've no business to do that without telling us,' I pointed out.

'Oh, you!' Babs turned away. 'You're mad because you didn't think of it first – that you didn't lend him Misty.' She looked across at Pam. 'Come on, Pam, let's see if your mother needs any help in the kitchen. We'll leave Jackie to cool off.'

CHAPTER SEVEN

BABS TAKES CHARGE

We had nearly finished lunch that day when the telephone bell rang. Babs immediately leapt from the table, still in the same annoyingly bossy mood.

'That might be for me,' she said while Pam and I exchanged glances. 'I expect it's Tim wanting to thank me for the loan of Patch.'

In her haste she left the door open and we were able to overhear.

'Yes, Tim, of course I meant what I wrote,' Babs was saying. 'No, I shan't have second thoughts . . . And I shan't really need Patch. I can always ride Misty.'

I almost choked on a mouthful of ginger pudding. There was no deterring Babs when she had one of her brain waves!

'But you must accept him,' she was protesting. 'Oh, don't take any notice of Derek and Giles. Of course, we won't be hanging around, getting in the way . . . All we want is for you to have a pony to ride until Robin's leg is better. Anyway, you'll be doing me a good turn . . . Patch needs a boy to ride him. He's a bit lazy, you know, and he feels he can get away with anything with me. You'll be doing me a good turn if you're strict with him.'

There was a pause and I could faintly hear Tim's voice over the wires. It seemed that he was still insistent on refusing the offer of Babs's pony. But would Babs let him?

'Just try him, Tim,' she coaxed. 'After all, it's a pity not to be able to practise for the Oakworth competition. Patch may not be as good as Robin, but at least he'll give you experience.'

Babs was quiet for a moment while it was Tim's turn to talk, but Babs just wasn't going to give him the chance finally to refuse.

'Oh, I can't stop to talk any more,' she declared firmly. 'I'm in the middle of lunch. I've got to go now. So you just keep Patch.'

I heard her determinedly replace the telephone before he could protest.

Babs came back into the dining room. 'There,' she announced. 'That's all settled.'

'Is it?' I said doubtfully.

Babs looked at me. 'What do you mean by that, Jackie?'

'Oh, nothing,' I said.

'You're not jealous, by any chance,' she challenged, 'because it's my pony that Tim will be riding instead of yours?'

'Don't be silly. Of course not.'

I lapsed into silence and kept out of my cousin's way for the rest of that day.

Next morning while Babs and Pam were attending to the ponies I took my spaniel – now well on the way to complete recovery – for a walk.

Outside the farmyard, I was in sight of Marlow's meadow, and my interest quickened as I saw, several hundred yards away, all three boys practising jumping. I stayed to watch, to see how Tim was managing on Patch.

Then I blinked in amazement.

Tim wasn't riding Patch. He was mounted on a blue roan.

Where was Babs's pony? What had happened?

Just then I wheeled round to hear the clomp-clomp of Babs and Pam, in wellingtons, hurrying towards me.

'I thought we'd find you here,' Babs challenged. 'What are you doing? Spying on the boys?'

'Oh, grow up,' I countered. 'I only happened to be passing, and they can't see me.'

'Well, it's too bad of you,' Babs persisted, 'when I'd told Tim that we wouldn't hang around –' She broke off as she caught sight of Tim on the strange pony. 'Good gracious, where's Patch?'

'That's what I've been wondering,' I said.

'Where have I seen that blue roan before?' said Pam puzzled. 'I know! It belongs to the Valley View Riding Stables. They sometimes enter it for gymkhanas. It's called Star.'

'It doesn't look as sturdy as Patch.' Babs could not hide her disappointment. 'I shouldn't think it's got much staying power.'

'Perhaps not,' I said. 'But I'm sure he's a lot more obedient than Patch.'

Babs flushed. 'How can you say that?' she demanded. 'You can't know. You can't judge in five minutes.' She started down the hill, calling over her shoulder: 'I'm going to telephone to find out what they're doing with Patch. Perhaps Tim wants to try them both, and then decide which to enter for the show.'

'You've got a hope,' I said under my breath,

and Pam and I followed my irrepressible cousin towards the farmhouse, dragging an unwilling Scamp behind us.

Barely had we reached the farmyard when we saw a small yellow sports car, pulling a pony trailer, coming up the lane. It stopped at the gate, and I saw, painted on the side of the trailer: VALLEY VIEW STABLES. A fair-haired girl of about nineteen got out. She was dressed in workmanlike jodhpurs, and a roll-necked, canary coloured sweater.

We walked up to her, mystified.

'Hello, Lynn,' said Pam. 'What are you doing here?'

'Delivering a pony,' the fair-haired girl said. She looked from Babs to me. 'One pony. Name of Patch. Which of you is the owner?'

Babs stepped forward. 'Patch is my pony,' she said, 'but there must be some mistake. Tim wouldn't mean you to bring him here. He probably wanted you to take him to the jumping field at your stables, so that he could try him over some proper jumps. That'll be it.'

The girl shook her head. 'Sorry, but there's no mistake.'

'Isn't there?' Babs said in a small voice, and I couldn't help feeling sorry for her. 'I'm not expecting Patch. What's happened?'

'Dr Emett rang me up himself after the boys had been over to hire one of my ponies,' said Lynn. 'The doctor said that he particularly wanted me to return Patch to you this morning. He said he was telephoning Mrs Wells to explain.'

I put a comforting hand on Babs's drooping shoulder. 'Cheer up, Babs.'

'Oh, leave me alone.' She shook me off. 'I expect you're really glad it's turned out like this.' She sank on the doorstep to pull off her wellingtons. 'Well, don't just stand there, Jackie. Get cracking. You haven't brushed Misty yet.'

'Fair enough,' I said peaceably, setting off towards the tack room, and wishing that Babs didn't sometimes get so touchy whenever one of her brain waves went wrong. In a way I was hating myself because I was somehow glad that Babs's plan had misfired.

'But what did Patch do wrong?' Babs demanded of Mrs Wells after Dr Emett had spoken to Pam's mother on the telephone later that morning.

'Quite a lot,' said Mrs Wells. 'When Tim went to get him out of the stable Patch played up. He nearly trapped Tim against the wall.

Then, when Tim did get him outside, and tried to ride him, Patch nearly threw him.'

'That's not like Patch,' said Babs. 'He may be wilful, but there's no vice in him.'

'That's true,' Pam said.

I nodded. 'Yes, but you know how being in strange surroundings upsets Patch. He was a bit difficult when we first came to Holly Farm.'

'True enough,' Mrs Wells continued. 'Apparently Derek went to help Tim to get Patch over one or two of the jumps, and Patch tried to kick him.'

'I can just imagine,' Babs said feelingly. 'That Derek! I expect he tried to frighten him into jumping. Patch would have settled down if Derek hadn't interfered.'

'Anyway,' Mrs Wells continued, 'Dr Emett saw what was happening from his surgery window, and he went out to stop it before anybody got hurt. He said that he didn't want to take the responsibility of any of the boys bringing Patch back. So he asked Lynn Harmon to bring him. He said he felt it would be best to get a professional to do the job, so that Patch would be returned safe and sound.'

'Poor Dr Emett!' put in Mr Wells, who had just come into the house, 'having to cope with

Patch, as well as his surgery, patients, Health Scheme and form-filling. I think the best turn that you girls can do those boys is to keep right out of their way.'

'I quite agree,' said Mrs Wells. 'Make your own fun without the boys. It's going to be a really hot day. Why don't you take a picnic and ride to the beach? Have a swim, and try to forget about the boys.'

'Good idea, Mummy,' said Pam. 'Because if we hang around the farm we can't help hearing them jumping in Mr Marlow's field. Let's make a firm resolution and keep to it. We're going to forget about the boys entirely. Put them right out of our minds.'

CHAPTER EIGHT

WE'LL SHOW THEM!

What a scorcher that day turned out to be!

The sun blazed down as we trotted along the lanes to the sea.

Our ponies were listless and plodded heavily through the loose sand of the dunes. Soon we were able to unsaddle them in the shade of Whale Rock while we changed into our swimsuits, and plunged into the lazy waves.

Half-an-hour later we changed back into our jeans and sports shirts, and rode the ponies through the shallows.

Patch made a fuss when the mushy sand squelched into his hooves. Babs was stern with him. She thwacked him with the end of her reins, and then gave him a sharp dig with her heels, taking him so much by surprise that he followed Misty and Strawberry into the shallows before he realized what he was doing.

The ponies splashed through the wavelets and we walked them right along the length of the beach. We had turned and were riding back when, to our amazement, we saw three other riders winding down through the sandhills to the shore.

'The boys!' gasped Pam, reining up Strawberry and staring. 'I suppose the heatwave made them decide to come to the beach, too.'

At that moment the boys saw us because they, too, halted, and seemed to hold a council of war.

'What are they going to do now?' wondered Babs.

'I hope they go somewhere else,' said Pam. 'How can we keep to our resolution if we're always going to run into them?'

We watched as the boys trotted their ponies towards the breakwaters beyond some fishermen's cottages.

'So that's it,' said Pam as we saw them line up their three ponies and canter towards the first of the breakwaters. 'They're not bothering to go away.'

'Yes I suppose they've decided just to ignore us,' I said.

Slowly we walked our ponies as the boys rode at the first jump. Tim's blue roan seemed to lag behind the other two. Uncertainly he heaved himself over the obstacle and cantered after Derek's and Giles's ponies to the next breakwater. He rapped it with his near hind. Then, rising too late for the next jump, he caught it with his forelegs. After that he refused.

'Some gymkhana pony, I don't think!' exclaimed Babs. 'Why, even Patch can do better.' She reined up, and looked at Pam and me challengingly. 'Let's show them what we can do. Are you game?'

Pam and I looked at each other. 'What about our resolution?'

'Blow our resolution!' said Babs. 'We'll show them.'

Impulsively I put Misty into a canter. 'Here goes,' I said, with some misgiving.

Pam lagged. Then Strawberry decided for her, and soon the three of us were cantering level towards our end of the breakwaters. Babs gave Patch a smack just to show him that she was going to stand no more nonsense. Our ponies took off together. We cleared two of the jumps. Then Patch drew across Strawberry throwing her off her stride. While Babs and Pam sorted themselves out Misty and I cantered on.

'Hey, what do you girls think you're doing?'

yelled Derek.

'Showing you boys how to jump,' Babs retorted cheekily.

Misty was jumping superbly, in and out of the line of breakwaters with never a false step. The schooling she had received while we'd been at Holly Farm had brought her to the peak of her form. Perfectly balanced and surefooted, she was jumping like a champion.

Misty and I reached the end of the breakwaters without a fault. As I reined up I stole a glance towards the boys who, now dismounted, were standing with their ponies, watching us. Were they surprised to see our prowess? I hoped so.

'Well done, Jackie,' Tim called to my astonishment.

I was about to put Misty over the jumps again when an idea struck me. I paused, and then screwing up my courage I made up my mind, and with cheeks flushing, but none the less determined, I rode over to the boys. It was now or never, I told myself. I'd make a final try to win their friendship.

'Would you like to jump Misty, Tim?' I offered, dismounting. 'She's reliable, not temperamental like Patch. Go on. Try her.'

The boys were taken off their guard by my

sudden action. Tim looked from me to Misty and then to Derek, and my heart sank as I saw Derek shake his head. Tim then looked towards Giles who just shrugged.

'Oh, why don't you decide for yourself, Tim?' I challenged, pushing the reins into his hands.

'I'm tempted,' Tim admitted with a rueful smile, and suddenly making up his mind he put a foot into Misty's stirrup.

'You must be bonkers,' Derek told him frankly. 'I've suspected it for some time.'

Tim lengthened the leathers a hole. Then, clucking encouragingly to Misty, he moved off, trotting up the beach, and cantering a circle to get the feel of her before starting to jump.

Misty jumped just as well for Tim as she had been doing for me. She took the breakwaters in her stride one after the other. As she landed after the last one, Tim reined up and patted her. Then he trotted across to us.

'Thanks very much, Jackie,' he said. 'She's certainly a grand pony.'

'Not bad,' conceded Derek to our surprise.

'We'd no idea that you girls could jump so well,' admitted Giles, emboldened by Derek's unusual pleasantness.

My spirits soared. I turned to the two more

difficult boys. 'Why not jump Misty as a three-some.'

'Even when she doesn't know the other ponies?' Giles queried, doubtfully.

'Misty's not fussy,' I said. 'Go on. See if she'll make up a team for you. You can use her as often as you like until Robin's better.'

'That's all very well,' said Derek after a moment's thought. 'But borrowing anyone else's pony is a big responsibility, as you should know, Jackie, after what you did to Robin – laming him.'

'I know,' I said, shamefaced. Why did he have to bring that up? 'That's why I want to make amends.'

'All the same,' said Giles as Babs and Pam rode up to join us, 'I do think you girls are apt to make rash offers.'

'Hear! Hear!' said Derek, and fixed me with a stern gaze. 'Just think what would have happened if Tim had accepted Babs's offer, and kept Patch. Quite apart from the fact that somebody might have got hurt, she'd soon have got fed up when she found herself ponyless. She'd have seen Tim riding her pony while she hadn't got a mount. What would she have done today for instance? You wouldn't all three have been down here on the beach enjoying yourselves.'

'Oh, yes, we would,' said Pam, 'because Tim could have lent Babs Star – Lynn's pony.' She nodded to the blue roan.

'Oh no, he couldn't,' Derek pointed out, 'because when we hired Star we had to sign an agreement undertaking not to sublet him or to loan him out.'

Babs looked impatient. 'You boys do make difficulties,' she said. 'We'd still have had Strawberry and Misty, and we could have taken turns to ride them, and if we'd wanted to go for picnics one of us could have ridden Pam's bicycle.'

'That's not the point,' said Derek. He looked at his watch. 'Anyway, I don't know why we're standing around here, wasting time, yackety-yacking, instead of getting on with our riding.'

'Don't worry about us so much, Jackie,' added Tim, perhaps considering my bruised feelings. 'There's no need for you to imagine that you've got to lend me Misty because of what happened to Robin. Ponies do have mishaps. It could have happened just as easily when I'd been riding him.'

'So forget it, for goodness' sake,' put in Giles, gathering up his reins, ready to mount Swallow, his bay. 'And let us all carry on with our own affairs.'

'You're not very friendly, are you?' Babs said, not wanting the boys to have the last word. 'After all, we're all pony people, and most pony people like to do things together.'

'And help each other out,' I added.

'Here endeth the first lesson,' groaned Giles.

Babs's eyes flashed. 'That's right; make fun of us. Just because you're boys, and a year or two older than us, I expect you think it's beneath your precious dignity to be bothered with us. If you were girls we'd all be having a jolly good time, having jumping competitions, schooling the ponies together and having super all-day rides and picnics. You boys make me wild.'

'Right,' said Derek, in a final way. 'Now we understand each other. You three go your ways and we'll go ours.'

'Speak for yourself, Derek,' protested Tim. 'I don't mind joining up with the girls. After all they've proved what good jumpers they are.'

'Well! Well! Sir Timothy Galahad!' Derek mocked. 'Right, Giles and I will go back to Marlow's meadow to do some proper jumping while you, Tim, play gymkhanas with your girlfriends.'

CHAPTER NINE

PONY DAY PLUS TIM

Leaving Derek and Giles gaping, Tim jumped
on to Star's back and put the blue roan into
a gallop. Babs, Pam and I scrambled into our
saddles and thundered after him.

When he'd gone about a hundred yards Tim
slowed down to give us a chance to catch up.
Then, as we all drew level, we set off again,
racing in earnest. Sand flew from our ponies'
hooves. The sea wind ruffled their manes and
made their tails stream. The blue roan might
not be much good at jumping, but he was a
speedy pony, and neither Misty nor Strawberry could keep up. Racing, however, was
one thing Patch didn't mind doing and he, too,
was fast. Leaving Pam and me behind, Babs and
Patch pounded after Tim.

Patch drew level, and, neck and neck with

the blue roan, reached Black Rock to finish the race in a dead heat.

'Well, done,' I panted as Pam and I caught up.

Laughing, we patted our ponies.

'That was terrific,' sighed Tim.

'Super,' agreed Pam, turning to Tim. 'It's much more fun riding with you, Tim. I'm glad you decided to team up with us. Think what wonderful times we can all have. We can have cross-country rides, treasure hunts, picnics, moonlight gallops. We might even organize our own point-to-point.'

'That would be wonderful,' I added, turning to smile at Tim.

'Yes,' Babs was going on, full of happy plans. 'Think of it – all the summer holidays ahead, day after day, and you can be riding all the time with us, Tim, instead of with that grumpy pair.'

I saw Tim's smile fade, and knew that, as often happened, Babs had said too much. I expect that the prospect of days and days in our company, riding with girls instead of with Derek and Giles, did not appeal to Tim quite as much as Babs had hoped.

'Not so fast,' said Tim, with a quick laugh. 'I can't leave Derek and Giles high and dry, you know. After all, Derek is my cousin and I do live at his house. I wouldn't have a home if it wasn't for Derek's mother and father. I'll still have to ride with Derek and Giles most of the time.' He paused. 'This is just a day off, so to speak – so let's make the most of it.'

Pam and Babs and I looked at each other and smiled.

Tim reined up and dismounting, piled up some branches of trees that had been washed up by the tide to make a jump, and our ponies found this easy after the breakwaters. Star just picked up his forelegs and popped himself over, and our ponies followed. Then we decided on a bending race – a zig-zag course, cantering in and out of a line of tall rocks. Willingly Misty responded to the aids as I set off down the course, weaving with supple ease in and out of the rocks, answering to the touch of the reins on her neck with the sensitivity of a polo pony.

'One minute, twenty seconds,' Tim said as I reined up beside him. 'Off you go, Babs.'

Patch bucked before he even started. Then, shaking his head against the bit, he declined to follow the course. Babs rode him back to the beginning, and started again. This time Patch overshot the second of the rocks, and had to start yet again.

'Don't give up hope, Babs,' Tim advised. 'Get him to walk it so that he realizes you're determined to make him do it right.'

Babs walked Patch in and out of the rocks. Then she trotted, and he jibbed, so Pam had to dismount and run beside him, her hand on his bridle.

At the next attempt Patch managed to finish the course to cheers although his timing wasn't worth recording.

'Thanks for being so patient, everybody,' said Babs, as Pam cantered Strawberry down the course and back to beat my time by five seconds.

Now it was Tim's turn, and though Star was sluggish Tim drove him forward and completed the course ten seconds ahead of us.

'Hurrah!' Babs cheered as Tim rode back to us. 'I bet you're enjoying yourself just as much as you did with Derek and Giles.'

'More,' Tim said with a grin. 'You're better sports.'

We glowed with pleasure. Tim was happy. All our efforts to make friends had not been wasted.

'What shall we do now?' said Pam. 'I know! Let's have a cross-country ride back to the farm.'

'Great,' said Babs.

'Sounds fine to me,' said Tim. 'A pipe-opening gallop and some natural jumps are just what Star needs to get him going.'

'And we'll be back at the farm in time for tea,' said Pam. 'Gosh! How the afternoon's flown! You'll stay and have tea with us, won't you, Tim?'

'I'd like that,' said Tim, as we moved off. He added to Pam. 'You lead. You know this line of country better than anyone.'

Pam took a winding path through the sand dunes and the other ponies followed. Then she set off at a canter that quickly became a gallop. Over the short turf we thudded. Even Patch and Star were excited now. I could see froth at the end of Patch's bit as he fought Babs, trying to overtake Pam and Strawberry.

'Hold him back, Babs!' called Tim. 'Let Pam keep the lead. She's the only one who really knows the way.'

We skirted a quarry and took our first jump – a low fence and ditch that edged a field of stubbly grass where the hay had not long been cut. Even Star jumped it well, not wanting to be left behind by the other ponies. Across the field we thudded. A stile lay ahead.

72

Misty pricked her ears eagerly. She loved jumping but, beside me, I could sense Babs's hesitation. She caught sight of a gap and rode Patch towards it.

'I'm going to make Star jump the stile,' panted Tim, drawing level with Misty and me. 'Give me a lead, Jackie.'

Misty needed no urging. She took off and sailed over the jump in her usual effortless fashion. Behind me I heard Star snort and looked back to see Tim leave the saddle and land halfway up the blue roan's neck as he refused. Tim struggled back into the saddle and rode Star at the stile again.

'Go on!' he urged, giving the blue roan a smack with the flat of his hand. 'Up!'

This time they were over and we thundered up the slope. We took the low hedge at the top and reined up as we saw Babs and Pam trying to hold their ponies steady amid a herd of inquisitive bullocks.

Patch squealed and shied, startling the bullocks, who charged. Babs swung him round to dodge them and the bullocks swerved after Pam and Strawberry.

'Come on!' Tim turned to me, urging Star forward. 'To the rescue!'

We cantered towards the bullocks, waving

73

our switches and shouting. The bullocks took one look at us and lurched in a jostling mass towards the corner of the field.

'Scram!' Tim yelled.

Our tactics were successful – too successful! The bullocks, driven by herd instinct, panicked and three of them broke through the hedge into the lane.

'This way,' I called, wheeling Misty towards the gate. 'Hurry!'

Babs and Pam joined us as we rode through the gate. We looped our ponies' reins through the second bar and left our mounts on the grass at the side of the lane, while we ran to herd up the bullocks.

Brandishing our switches and shouting we advanced. The bullocks began to trot farther down the lane.

Tim held up his hand to halt us. 'This won't do,' he declared. 'We're driving them farther away. Babs and Pam, stand on this side of the gap. Jackie – you come with me to outflank them.'

Babs and Pam stationed themselves in the lane, guarding one of the bullocks' exits. Meanwhile Tim and I climbed through into the opposite field and crept along the hedgerow out of sight of the bullocks.

'We've cut off their retreat,' panted Tim. 'Now for the tricky bit.'

We got into the lane, and advanced.

The leading bullock stopped with lowered head at the sight of us. Then he turned and, followed by the other two, charged towards Babs and Pam. Babs looked a bit scared. She always was rather afraid of cattle at close quarters; but Pam was a farmer's daughter and she gamely barred the way.

'I'll cope, Babs,' Pam shouted. 'Stand clear.'

Pam sidestepped neatly, and caught the charging bullock a whack on his quarters with her switch. He swerved and charged through the gap in the hedge, followed by the others.

'Well done,' said Tim, pleased, as we made up the broken hedge with branches. 'You saved the day, Pam.'

'Phew!' gasped Pam. 'I'm relieved to hear you say that, Tim. I thought you were going to blame me for leading you all into a field of bullocks, but I didn't know they were there. They've never been in this field before.'

'Yes,' said Babs. 'I thought we'd blotted our copybooks again. Some people would have been cross.'

'Derek for one,' I said feelingly. 'And probably Giles.'

'Oh, don't talk about them,' said Tim. 'It's doing me good to have a rest from them for a while. You three may be only girls,' he said with a grin, 'but you're jolly good sports. I haven't enjoyed myself so much for ages.'

CHAPTER TEN

WHEN BOYS FIGHT . . .

'I can understand why you girls have taken such a liking to Tim,' said Mrs Wells when Tim had, at last, left to go back to the Emetts' after tea and a romp with Scamp. 'He's such a pleasant, kindly boy.'

'Yes,' agreed Mr Wells, knocking out his pipe, and getting up from the armchair where he had been reading his newspaper before going on his usual evening round of the farm.

'He seemed to enjoy being here, too,' went on Mrs Wells, starting to clear the table. 'Strange really, because not many boys of that age would want to spend an afternoon with three girls. After all, it's not as if he's lonely. He's got plenty of company at the doctor's, with his cousin, and that other boy they've got staying there.'

'That's just the trouble, Mummy,' put in

Pam. 'Derek and Giles aren't really much company for Tim.'

'Derek's always getting at Tim,' I explained. 'I suppose he's jealous of him, and resents him coming to live with them.'

'Perhaps he doesn't like to share his mother and father with someone else,' said Mrs Wells.

'That's all very well,' said Babs, helping to pile up the plates. 'But Derek ought to try not to show it. After all, poor Tim's had enough trouble, losing his mother and father in that crash.'

'It's difficult for both of them,' said Mrs Wells understandingly, 'and I suppose Dr and Mrs Emett must find it rather uncomfortable to have the boys at loggerheads.'

'I don't suppose they know what's going on,' said Babs. 'Dr Emett's too busy to worry about anybody but his patients, and Mrs Emett is always out.'

'Yes, she's all for committees,' nodded Mrs Wells.

'That's just it,' said Pam. 'I expect she's so busy looking after other people's troubles, serving on the Marriage Guidance Council, and the Citizens' Advice Bureau and the Child Welfare Association, and goodness knows what else that she doesn't notice the problems in her own family right under her nose, so to speak.'

We were all thoughtful as we helped Mrs Wells with the dishes. I suppose we were wondering what we could do to help, but it was difficult. We'd have liked to ask Tim over to spend another afternoon with us, but we didn't want to seem pushing. Being girls it was difficult to do the right thing where boys were concerned.

We went out to the paddock to say good night to the ponies. Misty was the first to come trotting towards us through the summer twilight, and I stroked her nose as she lipped from my hand some pieces of carrot.

This was one of the best times of the day, the three of us there in the dusk with our ponies quietly munching while we made much of them.

Misty finished her carrot and nosed my pocket hopefully for more.

'That's the lot,' I told her. 'I don't want you to get too fat.'

She butted me with her head as though to say 'Spoilsport', and I almost lost my balance. I grabbed at her mane. I put my hand against her shoulder to steady myself and then, as I stepped back, I felt something hard under my foot, I bent down to look, and there, glinting in the evening light, was a small round bronze-coloured object – a Pony Club badge.

I put my hand to the lapel of my jacket. My badge was still securely in position.

'Is this yours?' I turned to Pam and Babs.

'No, I've got mine,' said Pam.

'And mine's in the house,' said Babs. 'The pin's bent so I left it on the dressing table.'

'Perhaps this belongs to Tim then,' I said. 'That's a bit of luck because now we have got an excuse to telephone him. We'll ask him if he's lost his Pony Club badge and, at the same time, try to sound him out about coming over again.'

We dashed indoors, and I picked up the telephone, and dialled the Emetts' number. To my dismay, it was Giles who answered, and this put me off my stroke.

'Hello, Giles,' I said apologetically. 'Sorry to trouble you. May I speak to Tim?'

'Just a minute.' Giles's voice sounded agitated. 'There's a bit of a flap on here. I wouldn't have answered the telephone, but I thought it might be a patient needing the doctor – oh, gosh!' He broke off to speak to other people. 'Steady on, you two. Oh, for goodnesssake, break it up!'

I heard a thud as though the telephone was being flung down. Then I heard voices in the background; grunts, and a shout; then Tim's voice came over the wires quite clearly but from a little distance: 'Be reasonable, Derek,' followed by Derek's: 'I'll show you!' There followed a clatter and a crash, a yell of pain, and silence, broken by Giles calling: 'Help! Why doesn't someone help. Dr Emett! Come quickly.'

I gripped the telephone, agonized.

'Giles!' I shouted into the mouthpiece. 'Whatever's happening? Answer me!'

Suddenly the telephone rattled, and I heard Giles's breathless voice saying into the mouthpiece: 'Oh, for goodnesssake, Jackie, get off the line!'

'What's wrong?' I demanded. 'Are Derek and Tim fighting? And what was that crash? Is Tim hurt?'

'Tim!' Giles echoed. 'Tim's all right. It's Derek I'm worried about. He's really injured.' He paused. 'I'll have to give some first-aid.' He broke off exasperatedly and then went on. 'It's your fault, Jackie. If you hadn't dragged me to the telephone I might have been able to break up the fight. Now I've got to pick up the pieces. *Goodbye*!'

There was a click as he put down the receiver and I was left blankly looking at the telephone.

I felt shattered. The end of Tim's happiest day – a fight with the cousin whose parents had taken him in. No doubt the cause of the trouble had been Tim riding off to spend the afternoon with us girls. Our fault, again!

CHAPTER ELEVEN

. . . AND GIRLS FALL OUT

'Something terrible's happened!'

I poured out my heart to Babs and Pam, but we were too horrified to tell Pam's mother and father. I suppose we did not want to say anything which would show Tim in a bad light.

We crept about next day, hanging around the house, hoping, yet dreading, that someone might telephone with news, but not daring to telephone ourselves in case we made matters worse.

'I'm sure Derek deserved whatever he got,' Babs said loyally. 'I'm quite sure he must have provoked Tim beyond endurance. Tim just isn't the type to lose his temper easily.'

I nodded, and looked out of the window yet again.

'We'd better school the ponies, or something,' said Pam. 'We can't just mope around the house all day. Otherwise Mummy and Daddy will suspect that there's something wrong.'

We caught the ponies, brushed and saddled them and then practised trotting and cantering in circles, and reining back. Misty and Strawberry backed easily, but Patch, as always, was obstinate. I had to dismount and stand in front of him, my hand on his reins near the bit, encouraging him until he moved back with his near hind and off-fore. Then I made much of him, and gave him a piece of apple before trying to get him to take another step backwards.

'Come on, Patch,' I urged, tapping his off-hind with my switch to get him to move. 'Be a good pony. You're not really as stupid as this, you know.'

Patch's heart was not in his lessons, and I suppose ours weren't either, although Pam and I went on to try to get Misty and Strawberry to perform the shoulder-in. That is, we were teaching them to move diagonally off-course, so to speak.

While we were trotting, the ponies had to bend their heads, necks and shoulders inwards, flexing so that their forelegs moved in a separate track, parallel to the original one. This was quite an advanced piece of training, and for a little while, took our minds off Tim and his problems.

All the same, we could not help being aware of the silence and emptiness of the boys' jumping field – no thud of hooves approaching the hurdles; no sound of boys' voices, or the neighs and stamps of ponies.

The day dragged on in an agony of suspense; and the night was even worse because, when I did sleep, I had anxious, unhappy dreams of Tim being lost in a thick mist, and my calling, trying to find him, and his voice getting farther away, and then hearing nothing except Derek's mocking laughter.

Next morning I was glad to be jerked from my troubled sleep by Babs shaking me.

'The boys are back in the meadow,' she said excitedly. 'Listen.'

Through the open window, I heard the sound of ponies galloping over turf, the thunder of hooves and the thud when a pony landed over a jump, all against a background of boys' voices.

Pam had already heard what was going on and she was standing in the bedroom doorway. I scrambled out of bed, and the three of us hurried up to the attic where, through a dormer window, we knew we would have a clear view of the jumping course and the riders.

To our dismay, when we got there and crowded round the window to look, we could see only two boys and only two ponies.

'Derek and Giles!' I exclaimed. 'Where's Tim?'

'Perhaps he's in disgrace,' said Babs. 'He might even have been stopped riding as a punishment – or been kicked out, never to darken the Emett door again.'

'Anyway, whether Derek was really hurt in the fight or not, he seems all right now,' Pam pointed out. 'Mind you, he might have been out of action yesterday.'

'I know Tim wouldn't really hurt him,' I said. 'I expect they had a scuffle, and Derek tripped over himself or something. It would be just like him to do a lot of moaning and groaning just to get Tim into trouble.'

'But where's Tim now?' said Babs. 'That's what I want to know.'

Just then we heard the click of the farm gate and saw the postman cycling away down the lane. A moment later, Mrs Wells's voice floated up the stairs: 'Letter for you, Jackie.'

I thought it was odd as I was not expecting a letter. I had had one from my parents the previous day. I ran downstairs and took the letter from the newel post where

Mrs Wells had put it. My hand trembled as I saw the unfamiliar handwriting. Could this be a letter from Tim? My heart missed a beat.

> *Cedar Cottage*
> *Moatsey.*

Dear Jackie,

Giles tells me that you had a sound-only version of a real-life TV type drama when you telephoned the other night. Not to worry, Jackie. It probably sounded worse than it actually was. It ended with Derek falling halfway down the stairs, and knocking himself out, the clot.

However, as you will see by the above address, I decided that there ought to be a 'cooling-off period' to enable normal relations with the Emett family to be resumed. So I have taken advantage of a long-standing invitation to stay with an old school friend of mine in a village about twenty miles away. You'll be pleased to know that Robin's lameness is now quite cured, so I've taken him with me: In fact I rode him over here.

Meanwhile happy jumping, and all the best to Pam and Babs, and Mr and

Mrs Wells, and thanks for a truly super pony day.

> *Yours,*
> *Tim.*

I waved the letter excitedly as I dashed back upstairs.

'Tim seems to be all right,' I told Babs and Pam who were waiting agog on the landing.

'What a relief!' said Pam, as she craned over Babs's shoulder to read the letter.

Babs did not react as I had expected. She was gazing at the letter with a hurt expression on her face. 'Dear Jackie,' she read slowly. '*Dear Jackie.*' She looked at me with a frown. 'What I can't understand,' she said slowly, 'is why he wrote just to you and not to all of us? We're all his friends, you know – not just you, Jackie.'

'I know,' I said, and added without thinking: 'Perhaps it's because he's seen more of me than he has of you and Pam, Babs.'

'So that's it,' said Babs. 'Now you think you're his special friend.'

'Oh, don't be silly, Babs,' I said, exasperated. 'What does it matter? Who cares who the letter's addressed to?'

'Suppose it had been addressed just: "Dear Babs",' countered my cousin. 'You'd have felt hurt then, wouldn't you?'

I didn't answer because I knew Babs was right. Yes, I suppose I would have felt – what? Jealous? Could well be.

'Oh, I don't know why you two are bickering,' broke in Pam. 'We can all three write a joint letter back to him. We'll do it straight away after breakfast so that it catches an early post.'

Babs wasn't mollified. Still slightly huffy, she said: 'And I'll write a separate letter. Just from me.'

'How soppy can you get!' I retorted and Babs's cheeks flushed. She flounced into the bedroom and slammed the door. I turned to Pam. 'The green-eyed monster rides again,' I said flippantly.

'Oh, be quiet, Jackie,' Pam said with surprising heat. 'You're as bad as Babs. Two of a pair!'

Babs hardly spoke to me after breakfast but I pretended not to care, or even to notice. I forced myself to think of Tim instead. All the same, Babs, avoiding my gaze and pointedly talking only to Pam, intruded into my thoughts.

Why did she have to spoil my pleasure in Tim's letter?

Of course, I ought I suppose to have been more pacifying, but would it have helped? Babs had been really hurt at being excluded from Tim's letter. All the same I couldn't help feeling annoyed. She was acting childishly and if she thought I was going to let her sulk and blame me when anything happened that didn't suit her, she was jolly well going to find out her mistake.

My cousin picked up Pam's copy of *Pony Magazine* which had just arrived and began to turn over the pages, passing it over to Pam to show her any articles and pictures which particularly took her fancy and pointedly excluding me. Well, if that was the way she wanted it! I shrugged and went from the room and into the yard. Taking a scoopful of pony cubes from a sack I went to the paddock and called Misty.

'There, my beauty!' I said as she walked across to the gate and stretched her neck over to lip up one of the cubes. 'Who cares if Babs does want to be difficult?' I rubbed the white star on her brow as she munched. 'We can have a good time on our own, you and I. I'll take you for a really super ride with lots of cantering and jumping and we won't have to be bothered with obstinate old Patch.'

Patch and Strawberry had been grazing at the far side of the paddock and now, hearing his name mentioned, Patch came cantering across the grass, snorting, not wanting to be left out of the handout of any titbits that were going. I suppose my annoyance with Babs transferred itself to her pony. 'Go away, greedy!' I said, moving to Misty's other side so that Patch could not reach the pony cubes.

I'm not quite sure what happened then but Patch must have tried to slip his head sideways between the bars of the gate, hoping to reach the cubes that way. Suddenly he gave a squeal and shook his head only to find that it would not move. It was tightly wedged between the top two bars of the gate.

Patch kicked his back legs into the air and then began to pull frantically, still squealing.

'Steady, Patch,' I tried to soothe him while I sized up the situation.

'Don't move,' I calmed, trying to keep Patch still. It was no use. Babs's pony was desperate as any pony might be in the situation. 'Keep still, Patch.' I climbed over the fence and stood beside him. 'Help! Somebody, *help*!'

I called at the top of my voice. 'Mr Wells! Pam! Babs! Come quickly!'

I knew Patch might break his neck if he kept trying so wildly to pull himself free.

Babs and Pam, hearing my shouts and Patch's squeals, came running to the scene.

Babs sized up the situation, glared at me, and snapped: 'Pull yourself together, Jackie. Try to be level-headed. Can't you see that this is an emergency? Try to be useful instead of shouting there hysterically, frightening poor Patch.'

'Don't be so priggish, Babs,' I retorted. 'I had to call for help.'

'Well, stand back now, and for goodness' sake be quiet,' said Babs, clambering over the fence.

Grasping Patch's mane, she said soothingly: 'Easy does it,' and to our amazement, easy *did* do it. Patch happened to move his head just in the right direction to enable himself to get free.

'There you are!' Babs said smugly. 'No need for panic. It only needed someone to keep calm.'

'It might have needed the top bar sawn in half, or the gate taken off its hinges before Patch dislocated his neck,' I pointed out. 'You freed him, Babs, by a sheer fluke.'

'Really, Jackie,' put in Pam, 'can't you give anyone credit for doing the right thing? Patch is free and unhurt. That's all that matters.'

'Quite,' said Babs, and bent to pick up the scoop with the remaining pony cubes. 'So this is how it happened. It was all your fault, Jackie. You must have been feeding Misty on her own, and Patch would be trying to get his share, and that's how he came to get his head stuck in the gate.' She turned to Pam, deciding to ignore me. 'Pam, let's saddle up and train Strawberry and Patch. We can reschool them. I'll put a pole on the ground for them to trot over.'

'That's about all Patch can do,' I couldn't resist saying. 'That pony must have an IQ of about minus thirty.'

'We'll ignore that,' countered Babs. 'Come on, Pam. There's no point in trying to reason with Jackie while she's in an awkward mood.'

Leaving them to it, I saddled Misty and rode off, intending to go for a gallop on the common, to disperse my rage. I wasn't going to let them spoil my day.

CHAPTER TWELVE

TEMPERS FRAY

On the way I passed Marlow's field. The jumps were set up ready, but Derek and Giles were nowhere around. On a sudden impulse I rode Misty up to the gate, lifted the catch and rode her into the field. The boys had made some super jumps. Some of them were quite high, and they had several really tricky ones – an in-and-out, a wall made of bales of straw with a row of turves on top, a post-and-rails with a drop on the far side, and a triple bar with a really good spread.

Misty had jumped so well on the beach the previous day, and was obviously on the top of her form, that I just had to try her over some really difficult obstacles.

Misty felt like jumping that morning. Eager to begin she fretted against the bit as I collected her for the first fence. It was a fairly easy one

– a gorse jump with a low bar on the take-off side, and Misty took it in her stride.

We cantered to the in-and-out and Misty jumped it neatly, tucking her forefeet well under her for the second part of the jump. Next we rode for the wall, which was high, but Misty couldn't do wrong that morning. She took off in good time, extended herself well, and cleared the jump, going on to fly over the bales of straw, and the turves, with a foot to spare.

The drop on the far side of the post-and-rails surprised her, and she gave an extra 'jump' in midair, springing well out but she landed sure-footedly enough to canter on to the triple. Misty liked jumps with a spread because they seemed to help her judgement. She extended herself beautifully, flew over the top bar, and landed. A clear round.

I bowed to an imaginary audience, patted Misty and set off at a canter round the field. Then, closing the gate carefully behind us, we turned into the lane and rode up to the common. We had a gallop and, as we pounded over the turf, my spirits soared. Misty was a really good pony, and all the schooling and practice she had had while we had been at Holly Farm had brought her right to the top.

I thought of Babs and felt hurt and indignant. Her obstinate Patch had been holding us all back, but why should I bother with them? Misty was a jumper in her own right, and the competition at Oakworth was not only for teams. There were ordinary jumping classes, too. I would enter my pony for the under-fourteen-two novices, and give her a chance to show what she could do. I'd get the schedule that afternoon, and I wouldn't say anything to Babs about it. Why should I? She'd only say that I was big-headed, and a show-off, just because Misty was a natural jumper when Patch could have been a jumper, too, if Babs had taken the trouble to train him properly, and not let him get away with his wilful behaviour.

After lunch I went out to the saddle room to wipe over Misty's bit and bridle. Babs was there, too, getting out Patch's kit, apparently ready to go for a ride.

'Going anywhere interesting?' I forced myself to ask because I suppose I was feeling guilty at keeping my own exciting plans a secret.

'What's that to you?' Babs said shortly. 'You're not really interested.' Before I could make any reply she walked out, making it quite plain that she didn't want to have anything more to do with me.

I was seething. I'd offered the olive branch and Babs had brushed it aside. She was in the wrong now – not me. Feeling choked up, I was putting Misty's bridle away on its peg when Pam came in to get an egg basket.

I turned to pour out my heart to her. 'Really, Babs is the end. I'm ashamed of her – a cousin of mine behaving like this when your mother and father have been kind enough to ask her to stay.'

Then I stopped, noticing how quiet Pam had been while I was talking. Two spots of colour glowed in her cheeks as she forced herself to look straight at me. Her voice sounded strangled as she spoke at last.

'You're our guest, too, Jackie, and it's no use your thinking that I'm going to listen to you running down Babs. I'm just not going to take sides.'

'Take sides!' I echoed. 'It sounds to me as though that's just what you are doing, blaming me – just like you did this morning. Why don't you tell Babs all this?'

'That's just what I did,' Pam said, trying to be calm, 'about ten minutes ago.'

'Oh, did you?' I retorted. 'And what had

she got to say? Plenty of things about me, I expect.'

'I told her what I've told you,' said Pam. She lined the bottom of the egg basket with hay, and went to the door. 'Anyway I'm only sorry that I've got to go out with Mother this afternoon to see Aunt Jane in hospital, instead of staying around here to keep the peace between you and Babs.' She turned to me. 'You know, the trouble with you two is that you're as bad as one another. As I've told you before you're two of a pair!'

Pam went off towards the house while I, feeling more indignant than ever, went to the bus stop. I had decided to go to Valley View Stables. Lynn Harmon was secretary for the Oakworth show, and I wanted to get the schedules and enter Misty. I'd jolly well show them all, Babs and Pam, and Derek and Giles.

The bus came, and I climbed aboard and took a seat by the window. As we bowled along, I could see Marlow's field and the jumps; the common where I'd so recklessly, and selfishly, been showing off on Tim's pony Robin and lamed him; the vet's surgery outside which Mrs Windall had taken Robin from me, and said that Tim, obviously not trusting me to do any more harm would fetch the pony home himself. We passed Dr Emett's surgery where I'd gone full of good intentions to deliver my note offering Tim a share in Scamp, and where, due to my carelessness in not putting on his lead, Scamp had been kicked by Derek's pony.

Painful memories – it was all a horrible muddle.

The holiday that Babs and I had embarked on with such enjoyment at Holly Farm had become clouded with bad luck and anxiety, and now I had quarrelled with my cousin. Of course we'd had disagreements before, but never anything as serious as this. As these thoughts went through my mind, my enthusiasm for entering Misty for the Oakworth jumping faded, and I felt utterly miserable.

When the bus approached the Valley View Riding Stables I saw Lynn Harmon's pony trailer in a corner of the yard, and suddenly my mind was made up. As I alighted from the bus, and crossed the road to the stables I knew what I was going to do. There was no point in staying any longer at the farm, making things unhappy for Pam and uncomfortable for her mother and father who had been so kind. Perhaps if I went home, Babs and Pam would be able to enjoy themselves. They'd probably forget about the boys and go for happy rides and picnics. Babs would train Patch, muddling along somehow.

By a lucky chance Lynn Harmon was at home. She was in the tack room, cleaning a bridle.

'Hello, Miss Harmon,' I greeted, entering the tack room to join her. 'I wonder if you could do me a favour.'

'Certainly,' said Lynn Harmon, with a smile, 'if I can.'

I was just about to tell her that I wanted to book up the trailer to take Misty and me home next day when the telephone bell rang.

'Excuse me a minute.' Lynn made an apologetic *moue* and lifted the instrument. 'Hello,' she said into the mouthpiece. 'Valley View Riding Stables here. Yes . . . You'd like to book the trailer? When? Tomorrow? Well, yes, I can manage that.' My heart sank. I knew Lynn had got only one trailer. What bad luck that just as I'd been about to ask Lynn to take Misty and me home next day, somebody had rung up and pipped me at the post. It seemed so strange I could hardly believe it. Yet there was Lynn, pencil poised in hand, entering up the details in her appointments book. 'Where to?' she was saying. 'And what time would you like me to call? Very well . . . Yes, I've got all that . . . Thank you . . . Goodbye, Miss Spencer.'

Miss Spencer? I pondered. Then the penny dropped. Barbara Ariadne Bettina Spencer – Babs, no less.

Lynn turned to me as she put down the instrument.

'That was your cousin on the telephone,' she told me.

'I know,' I said, 'or rather I *guessed*. I didn't know she was going to fix up about a trailer. She never told me that she was planning to go home. As a matter of fact I was intending to do the same. That's why I'm here.'

'To book a trailer?' queried Lynn, looking slightly baffled.

'Yes,' I answered. 'I suppose I shan't be needing it now.' I tried to sort out my thoughts as I walked to the door. Two of a pair, Babs and me! Both of us had reacted to the unhappiness in the same way – *flight*. Suddenly the foolishness of the situation struck me. Babs and I had been good friends all our lives. We had spent super holidays together, and had wonderful pony times. Now, just because of a silly quarrel over Tim all that had been spoiled, and I knew that if either of us went home without making up the rift things would never be the same again.

At the door I turned. My mind was made up.

'Babs won't be needing that trailer, either,' I told Lynn. 'It's all a misunderstanding. We had a squabble, and haven't been speaking to each other. It made both of us miserable. I suppose that's why we both wanted to go home. Anyway, it's silly because really we're the very best of friends, and the sooner we make it up the better.'

Lynn's look of concern changed to an understanding smile.

Without saying anything, she took up the telephone and dialled a number.

'Valley View Riding Stables here,' she said into the mouthpiece. 'Is that you, Miss Spencer?'

'Yes,' came Babs's surprised voice over the wires.

Then, without saying anything more to Babs, Lynn handed me the telephone: 'It's all yours, Jackie.' She went out of the tack room, and quietly shut the door.

Words poured from me. 'Listen, Babs,' I said. 'Don't ring off. I'm terribly sorry that we quarrelled. Let's make it up. I didn't know that you were unhappy, too, until Lynn told me just now that you were planning to go home. This proves that we ought always to be good friends. You see, like Pam says, we are two of a pair because I was going to do the same thing, and the reason I couldn't book the trailer was because you'd already booked it.'

Relief surged over me as Babs broke into laughter. 'And I suppose you were feeling that Pam was fed up with you, too, just as I was because she kept on telling me off, and then saying piously that she wasn't going to take sides.'

'Well, we'll show Pam that we're not small-minded,' I declared. 'We'll all be real friends from now on.'

CHAPTER THIRTEEN

A SURPRISE FOR TIM

I was standing at the bus stop, impatient to get back to Holly Farm and Babs, when a grey car pulled up and Dr Emett offered me a lift.

'The bus has gone, Jackie,' he said. 'It passed me about three minutes ago when I was getting back into the car after making a call in the village. My next case takes me past Holly Farm, so you can come with me, if you like.'

Thinking how much more friendly Dr Emett was than his son, Derek, I was about to open the passenger door of the car when Dr Emett warned: 'Careful how you get in. Don't let the puppy escape.'

'Puppy,' I gasped, pushing back the wriggling, damp-nosed golden bundle that fawned at me as I climbed in. 'Oh, he's just like Scamp was when I first had him. I didn't know you'd got a dog, Dr Emett.'

'He's not mine,' said Derek's father. 'It belongs to one of my patients, but she's in need of a holiday to complete her convalescence, and this is the last of the litter. My patient can take the mother dog with her to her sister's where she's going to stay, but she felt she couldn't impose too much on her sister's good nature by taking a leaky puppy. So, to make sure that she gets her holiday which she needs, I said we'd look after the pup.'

'Tim would be pleased if he was at home,' I said, fondling the puppy's floppy ears as it clambered into my lap. 'It's just like his Goldie must have been when Goldie was a puppy.'

'So it is.' Dr Emett's kindly face looked troubled. 'I'd forgotten about Tim's own spaniel. I oughtn't to have forgotten, but I suppose I've got so much to think about.' His brow furrowed, and he went on as though thinking aloud: 'Is it a good idea, I wonder, to take the puppy home and risk bringing all that tragedy back into Tim's mind when he comes home?'

He drew the car into a lay-by. 'Perhaps I'd better take the pup to the kennels after all.'

'Oh, no,' I said, as the puppy nuzzled nearer to me. 'Tim will like the puppy. I know he will. It will be a comfort to him. Scamp was when he was at your house, even though Scamp was so ill, and we were all worried about him. Tim liked having him there. He was happier when he was with Scamp.'

'Yes, so he was,' said Dr Emett. 'I know Tim hasn't been as happy with us as he might have been, Jackie. Derek and he haven't exactly hit it off together. I suppose my wife and I ought to have taken a hand to try to smooth the way for them but we've both been so busy. We've just been waiting and hoping things would sort themselves out.'

'I suppose Derek's a bit jealous of Tim,' I said, trying to sound tactful. 'Tim's coming may have put Derek's nose out of joint.'

'Yes, but Derek's old enough not to behave so childishly,' Dr Emett said. He seemed to be speaking his thoughts aloud now, making up his mind to action. 'Tim has a great sorrow in his young life and it's up to all of us to make things easier for him. I'm going to have a word with Derek when I get home.'

I knew what would help Tim more than anything, but dare I say it? After all Dr Emett was a grown-up, and who was I to give advice? 'The puppy would help Tim to settle down, I'm sure,' I suggested hopefully. 'Couldn't you buy him for him as a present, Dr Emett? After all the litter must have been for sale.'

'Yes it was.' Dr Emett spoke shortly and I wondered if I had gone too far. Then to my relief he went on decisively. 'You're quite right. I'll buy the pup and I'll ring Tim up and tell him about it. Yes, that should probably do the trick. Thanks for having such a good idea, Jackie.'

'Tim's back!' Pam burst into the tack room two days later to tell us the news. 'He's riding up the lane on Robin, right now. He seems to be coming here.'

Babs and I dropped the leather we had been cleaning and rushed out into the farmyard just as Tim trotted through the gateway.

Tim had a duffle bag over his shoulder and from it was blinking an eager-eyed, silky, golden cocker spaniel puppy.

'Welcome home, Tim,' I said. 'I'm glad to see you've solved the problem of carrying your puppy around by pony.'

'Yes, he doesn't seem to mind,' said Tim, dismounting and lifting the puppy out of the bag to put him down on the cobbles at our feet. 'I think I've got you to thank for Bundle, Jackie,' he smiled. 'Uncle Roger told me that he'd never have thought of buying him if you hadn't advised it.'

As we played with Bundle, Scamp, hearing the puppy's delighted yap-yap, came bounding from the house to join in the fun.

'I thought they'd get on well together,' said Tim. 'Would you mind if I left Bundle here to play with Scamp while I join Derek and Giles in some jumping practice? They're in the meadow now. We want to make up for lost time so that we can still have a bash at the Oakworth.'

'Good for you,' said Babs. 'We'll keep an eye on Bundle.'

Several times after that, Tim left his puppy with us while the boys practised jumping. This led to the dogs becoming great friends, and we were not really surprised when, some days later, Tim telephoned and told us that Scamp had been seen that morning playing with Bundle in the Emetts' orchard. Scamp must have decided that instead of waiting for Bundle to be brought to play with him, it was high time that he paid a call on the puppy.

'That was nearly four hours ago,' Tim explained. 'And they haven't been seen since. Has Scamp come back to the farm?'

'No, we haven't seen him since breakfast time,' I said. 'Oh, dear. What can have happened? I don't think Scamp would have led him off anywhere. He's never shown any inclination to do so when he was playing with him here.'

'Well, we don't want to flap unduly,' said Tim, 'but I think we ought to organize some kind of a search.'

'We'll help, of course,' I declared. 'Where shall we meet?'

'Here, with the ponies in twenty minutes.'

CHAPTER FOURTEEN

A HECTIC SEARCH

Derek and Giles, already mounted, were waiting with Tim outside the Emetts' gate as Babs and Pam and I rode up.

'Thanks for letting us help, Derek,' said Babs, evidently deciding that a friendly approach to Tim's cousin might smooth the way ahead.

'Don't thank me,' said Derek, with a shrug. 'It was Tim's and Giles's idea. I was outvoted.'

'Before I telephoned you we'd already had a quick look round the house and in the immediate vicinity,' explained Tim. 'But I think we ought to cover the same ground again – round the garden on foot, and then split in six different directions, and muster, with any news, at the old windmill in, say, half an hour.'

My direction took me towards the main road and after dismounting to look in a culvert, and then behind a tumbledown wall, I was about to ride past the roadman's hut in the lay-by when I suddenly noticed something different about that hut.

I'd ridden past it yesterday, with Babs and Pam, on our way to the beach. The door had been hanging open with the hinges strained, and I'd thought that vandals must have broken in. Now the door was shut, but the padlock was on the ground. Somehow that seemed strange.

I dismounted to investigate, and when I was within a few feet of the door I knew I was hot on the scent. I heard a scrabble of puppy claws against wood, followed by a series of yelps.

'Oh, Bundle,' I exclaimed, pushing open the door of the hut and stooping to pick up the wriggling puppy, 'you must have strayed off, decided to look inside this hut, and somehow got yourself shut in. You are a pickle.'

The puppy's pink tongue dabbed my cheek as if to show how grateful he was to be rescued. I made a fuss of him and then shouted, at the top of my voice to let the others know that he had been found.

'Well, that's that,' said Derek. 'Mission accomplished.'

'What about Scamp?' said Tim, looking at

me. 'Is he still missing, or isn't he? We'd better check. It won't take a minute to telephone.'

When I spoke to Mrs Wells on the surgery telephone, she said that Scamp was nowhere around the farm, and that she would telephone the Emetts if he did turn up.

'Right,' said Tim when I reported to the others. 'The search goes on.'

'And as eldest boy, I think it's time I took charge,' decided Derek. 'We've got to plan this scientifically. We'll split up into pairs, and I suppose each of us boys will have to go with one of you girls if we're going to get any sensible results.' He looked round at us without enthusiasm. 'Babs had better go with Giles because he's strong-minded enough not to be misled by any of her scatty brainwaves. Pam's reasonably sensible so she'll be all right with Tim.' He paused and then glanced, with pained resignation towards me. 'That means I – heaven help me! – am to be landed with you, Jackie.'

The others trotted in their different directions, and Derek and I cantered across the field to the bluebell wood.

'Trust your dog to cause all this panic,' Derek grumbled as we dismounted, and then started to search. 'You girls don't train your animals properly.'

I said nothing. Apart from the fact that I did not want to upset Derek, I was uneasy about Scamp. He'd never been missing for so long. What could have happened to him?

We combed the wood, looking into thickets, probing the bracken and brambles with our switches, and peering into ditches and gullies, but without finding any trace of my missing spaniel.

Satisfied that Scamp was nowhere in the wood, we got back on to our ponies, and set off across the fields, taking one hedgerow each, and working our way thoroughly round the boundary of each before meeting and riding through the gateway into the next enclosure.

It was past tea time when we reached open moorland, and began to quarter it criss-cross. I was hoarse with calling my spaniel's name. Then, as I shouted to him, yet again, I imagined I heard an answering whimper. It seemed to come from an old lead-mine shaft. I reined up, and shouted: 'Scamp!'

Sure enough, there came an answering bark, followed by frantic whining.

'Derek,' I called. 'I've found him. He's fallen down the lead mine.'

We tied our ponies to a rowan trunk and hurried on foot to the disused mineshaft. We craned over. Six feet below, on the ledge of rock, just above the water was Scamp, wet and bedraggled, but apparently unhurt.

He scrabbled at the steep, slippery sides of the shaft in a vain attempt to reach us. His stubby tail wagged gamely as he yelped.

'Oh, poor Scamp,' I gasped. 'He must have fallen into the water, and then swum to the ledge. How are we going to get him out? I know! We'll buckle the reins together, and I'll fasten them round my waist, and go down to get him.'

'Oh, no, you won't,' said Derek. 'Trust you to want to play the heroine.'

'And trust you to start arguing,' I retorted, wishing that it had been Tim, not Derek, who had been nearby at the crucial moment, 'just as there's a job to be done.'

'Yes,' he grunted. 'But a job for a boy, not for a bit of a girl.'

Derek got the ponies' reins, buckled together the leathers and buckled one end of the reins to form a loop which he slipped over the sturdiest tree stump. He then fastened the other end round his waist, and prepared to go over the side while I rushed forward to hold the reins and take the strain of the leather.

'Leave it all to me,' Derek said tersely. 'I shall feel safer without your so-called help.'

I watched as, gripping the leather of the reins with both hands, Derek went over the edge of the shaft backwards, using his feet to fend himself off the sides. Below, Scamp reared up to yap a frantic welcome to his rescuer. I craned forward as Derek lowered himself to the ledge and bent to pick up Scamp.

Scamp was wriggling in Derek's arms and twisting his head to give Derek's face a grateful wash with his tongue. 'Keep still, Scamp,' Derek said, trying to hold my dog with one hand while, with the other, he looped the reins round his foot to form a stirrup on to which he could trust his weight and which would give him enough height to hand Scamp up to me.

Lying full length at the edge of the shaft, I stretched my arms down to grasp Scamp as Derek, one hand on the rope, made a superhuman effort to lift my dog above his head with the other.

Scamp, trying to help himself, scrabbled at the side of the shaft with his paws. He nearly toppled out of Derek's grasp, but I managed to grab his collar just in time.

Half-choking him in the attempt I jerked him on to the overgrown grass at the side of the shaft, and then got to my feet to try to help Derek.

'Stand clear,' he called. 'I'm going to hoist myself out.'

'I'll give you a hand.' I rushed to his aid, just as Derek scrambled on to the slippery edge of the shaft. We collided and – to my horror – Derek with a startled shout toppled backwards into the shaft.

There was a splash. Then silence.

I craned over the edge. 'Derek, are you all right?'

His voice was an enraged splutter. 'Oh, yes. I'm soaked to the skin, plastered in mud, and probably permanently disabled. Apart from that everything's great, you clot.'

CHAPTER FIFTEEN

LOSERS – BUT HAPPY

I hugged Scamp tightly, while Derek hoisted himself to the top of the shaft. He seemed to have difficulty in clambering over the edge, and I set down Scamp and stepped forward to take his arm.

Derek shook me off. 'Let go, can't you? What are you trying to do? Push me back in there again?'

'Oh, Derek, I'm so sorry.'

'Not half as sorry as me! Ouch!'

'You're hurt,' I gasped. 'Thank goodness I know a bit about first-aid.'

'No, you don't. Don't touch me.' Derek backed in alarm, gingerly putting his hand to his left shoulder. 'Keep away.'

With muddy water streaming down his face and clothes, he staggered towards his pony. I watched appalled as, with one hand, he tried to unhitch his pony's rein from the fence. He winced and fumbled, simple though the job was.

I rushed forward and pulled the loop free.

'That's one job I could have done if you'd given me the chance,' he said bitterly. 'Very well. You'll have to take over. I've sprained my shoulder and I can't get into the saddle. Button up my jacket, so that I can tuck my hand in it. Now lead my pony home for me.'

Meekly I obeyed.

'Come on, Scamp,' I bade.

During the whole of that miserable trek to Hilton Rise, Derek spoke only once:

'I suppose you realize that this puts paid to Tim, Giles and me entering as a team in the Oakworth competition. You've finally spoilt everything for us, and I hope you're satisfied.'

The thought of Derek out of action with a sprained shoulder through rescuing Scamp lay heavily on my conscience. I couldn't get Derek out of my mind. Worse, I kept thinking of Tim's and Giles's disappointment at no longer being able to compete in the Oakworth for which they had put in so much hard practice. On a sudden impulse I telephoned Tim, and suggested that

Misty and I took Derek's place and made up the team.

'Of course I know I'm not nearly as good as Derek,' I said. 'But Misty's a good jumper, and we might manage to get round the course. It seems such a pity for you and Giles to have to scratch because Derek's out of action.'

'I'll have to sound out Derek and Giles about this,' said Tim. 'Can I ring you back?'

'Yes, and I'll cross my fingers for luck,' I told him.

'You've got a hope,' Babs summed up as I turned from the telephone. 'All you'll get is cheek, or a snub.'

'Well, at least I'll have tried,' I said, and went to do some tack cleaning which I usually find soothing. But, though I worked busily, I was still tense with suspense by the time the telephone rang.

'It's okay by Giles and me,' came Tim's voice over the wires, and Babs, overhearing, pretended to faint with surprise. 'Derek said he couldn't care less. So there it is. Are you still game?'

I was feeling very jittery that afternoon as I rode Misty down to Marlow's field for a jumping practice with Tim and Giles, but my pony was raring to go. She enjoyed the company of other ponies, and being a good jumper liked, I think, to show off.

We did a round on our own, so that we could get used to the obstacles, while Tim and Giles watched. Of course we'd jumped most of them before, but the boys did not know this. So, in spite of me, in my nervousness, snatching at Misty's mouth, and making her get her timing wrong for the in-and-out, we did not do too badly.

It was a different matter, however, when Tim and Giles joined us and we all three tried to jump together. Tim's and Giles's ponies were slightly bigger than Misty, and they had more 'blood' in them, so they were having to hold them in to keep level with Misty while I was having to push her right up to keep pace with them.

To make matters worse, Swallow (Giles's pony) seemed to have caught Derek's and Giles's mistrust of the female sex, and every time Misty and I drew near him, he laid back an ear, and seemed to curl his lip at her. My pony got indignant, and hotted up.

After three rounds Giles reined up in despair and, glancing back at the shattered course, said: 'It's no use, Tim. It's ridiculous to think of our entering for the competition with Jackie instead of Derek. Our team will be a laughing stock.'

Tim's lips set. 'We're not giving in now,' he declared. 'As long as Jackie's game enough to carry on, we'll have a go.'

I didn't feel very game when the great day dawned, and it didn't help that Babs and Pam were now trying to pretend that everything would be all right. With sinking heart, I met the boys in the village to hack to Oakworth. Even Tim was quiet, feeling the strain, and matters were not improved when a furniture van thundered past and Misty, in backing, brushed against Swallow, who gave her a long-planned nip, sending her skittering across the road, nearly under the wheels of an oncoming car.

To add to my chagrin, when we got to Oakworth, there was Derek, among the spectators. His wrist was in a sling, and he had a cynical expression on his sallow face, obviously having at last made an appearance with the sole purpose of gloating over my final humiliation. He would be there to see the inevitable – my letting down Tim and Giles, and our having to retire from the jumping, thoroughly routed, to muted jeers from the spectators.

Misty was excitable. She had not been to a pony gathering for some time, and the presence of all the other ponies, the spectators taking their places along the course and the revving of cars into the car park, made her dance. There was a toot on a horn and I turned, trying at the same time to prevent Misty from backing into a hunter which was waiting for the adult competitions, to see the Wells's estate car. Mrs Wells was at the wheel and Babs and Pam craned through the window cheering me on while Scamp jumped from the back seat to the front, barking a greeting.

'It's up to us now,' said Tim, as our number was called, and he, Giles and I rode our ponies towards the start of the jumping course which was cross-country like a hunter trial.

We cantered to the first fence, a plain brushwood obstacle with a ditch on the take-off side, and all three ponies cleared it. The ground was rather soft after heavy rain in the night, and the previous competitors had churned up the going. As we galloped to the next fence, Giles's pony slipped, recovered and came crosswise at the jump, making Tim check Robin who also skidded, cannoning into Misty.

'Jinxed!' exclaimed Giles. 'Right from the start.'

'Be quiet, you clot,' warned Tim, and gave me an encouraging nod as we turned our ponies to ride at the jump again.

'Probably four faults!' countered Giles.

I felt myself going tense. How could I do well when I was so nervous, so dreading every fence ahead? What a fool I'd been to enter.

Misty sensed my uncertainty, and for the next two obstacles, took charge, cantering at them just right and popping easily over. Then the water jump lay ahead, and Misty faltered. I saw her left ear flick backwards as though to say: 'What do you want me to do now?'

I panicked, the reins going slack in my hands.

'Buck up, Jackie. You can do it,' Tim panted, trying to give me more room.

My hands clumsily shortened the reins – too tightly. Misty slithered to a stop just as Giles and Tim took off.

'Go on, Misty,' I urged desperately, clapping my heels to her sides. From a standstill my pony heaved herself forward. With an effort she landed with her forefeet clear but her back legs well and truly in the water.

'Another four faults,' mouthed Giles, as he and Tim paused for us to catch up.

'Whoops, dearie!' called a mocking voice,

and I saw Derek, wrist in sling, right in the front of a group of spectators. 'Next stop: Horse of the Year Show. What a splash you'll make. Ha! Ha!'

I glared. Horrid boy. A suspicion surged over me. Had Derek and Giles agreed when Tim suggested letting me join the team for the cruel pleasure of seeing me make myself an utter fool?

I glared at Derek, I'd never seen him look so pleased. That made me madder than ever. Somehow – I'll never know quite how – Misty and I sailed over the next jump and, level with Tim and Giles, we thundered towards a stone wall. I was keyed up. Derek's mocking face haunted me. I'd show him. I urged Misty right up into her bit. But what was the use? I'd never make it. Never. The wall looked so solid. I turned my head to blot out the frightening sight and instead saw Tim's freckled, mud-spattered face, his mouth set tensely. He was as keyed-up as I was. Perhaps a bit scared, too.

'We're not beaten yet,' I called above the pounding of our ponies' hooves, and shortening my reins I urged Misty to the take-off. She made a big effort, cleared it, and then we were galloping to the sheep hurdle, trying to make up for lost time.

Misty wasn't expecting the drop on the far side of the hurdle. She stumbled on landing. She managed to recover and we set off again half a length behind.

'Come on, Misty,' I called to her. 'Catch up.'

Ahead lay a triple post and rails; Misty sailed over it. Then I heard an ominous clatter, and glanced round to see Giles's pony picking its way out of the fallen jump, a victim of wrong timing.

I wasn't the only one who could make a mistake, I thought ruefully, as we raced for a small bank with rails on top. We all three managed this one, and set off downhill for the ditch that lay at the bottom.

We checked our ponies and cantered down the slope, collected them in time, and were safely over, and galloping towards the final post-and-rails. Misty and Swallow sailed over, but Tim's Robin took off too late and rapped the jump with his forelegs, bringing down the rail.

As we trotted off the course, Misty whinnied so that I wasn't even able to hear how many faults were announced over the loudspeaker. It didn't matter. There were so many of them.

Now for the moment of reckoning: Derek's scorn. He was coming towards us. He put a hand on Misty's bridle and turned to favour me with a blank stare instead of his usual scowl.

'So you lost count of the faults, eh?' he said tactlessly.

'Oh, don't rub it in,' I snapped. 'Go on. Laugh! That's what you want to do. You're a horrid boy.'

'And you're no Pony Club pin-up,' Derek countered, and then he saw my defeated look – I'd lost all my fight for the moment – and he suddenly dried up, shrugged, and after a while said: 'Oh, gosh! Why do we always have to fight? It's easier to be boorish to you than polite, Jackie, but I couldn't help feeling just a particle of sympathy during the last few minutes of the jumping.'

'What?' I gasped, hardly able to trust my hearing. Was Derek actually trying hard to be pleasant?

'Yes,' he went on. 'At least you were game, and everything considered you didn't really do badly. Not badly for a girl.'

'Oh, you!' I flashed. 'Boys! Girls! You'd think we lived on different planets. Well, I'm not going to stand here arguing with you. I'm dying for a lemonade.'

'You can treat me,' Derek said.

'Gallant, aren't you?' I walked off, and I was surprised when he followed me.

After we'd gone about twenty paces, Tim joined us. He fell in step beside me, and Derek walked on ahead.

'Thanks, Jackie,' Tim said quietly.

'What for?' I asked.

'For being such a good loser – and, oh, for everything.' He smiled at me. 'You wanted to help me, and you did, and that's the truth. Cheer up! Don't you understand? We can all be happy now.'

I looked at Tim. Could we all be happy? Was Derek really going to overcome his jealousy? Had he perhaps even begun to feel sorry for us when we were trying our best in spite of all our bad luck in the jumping? Did he now feel some respect and friendliness instead of envy and anger?

'Hurry up, you lot,' Derek called from the entrance of the refreshment tent where he was now standing with Giles. 'It's my treat.'

'Wonders never cease,' said Pam, staring hard at Derek and seeing just the faintest flicker of a smile. 'Who'd have thought that he'd have such a change of heart if that's what he has had? Or, of course, he might just be sickening for something.'

'All's well that ends well,' hopefully summed up Babs, linking arms with Tim and me. 'Although, of course, nothing can ever go completely right all the time – not when ponies are around. But I suppose that's more than half the fun.'

Home Farm Twins
JENNY OLDFIELD

66127 5	Speckle The Stray	£3.50	❏
66128 3	Sinbad The Runaway	£3.50	❏
66129 1	Solo The Homeless	£3.50	❏
66130 5	Susie The Orphan	£3.50	❏

All Hodder Children's books are available at your local bookshop or newsagent, or can be ordered direct from the publisher. Just tick the titles you want and fill in the form below. Prices and availability subject to change without notice.

Hodder Children's Books, Cash Sales Department, Bookpoint, 39 Milton Park, Abingdon, OXON, OX14 4TD, UK. If you have a credit card you may order by telephone – (01235) 831700.

Please enclose a cheque or postal order made payable to Bookpoint Ltd to the value of the cover price and allow the following for postage and packing:

UK & BFPO – £1.00 for the first book, 50p for the second book, and 30p for each additional book ordered up to a maximum charge of £3.00.
OVERSEAS & EIRE – £2.00 for the first book, £1.00 for the second book, and 50p for each additional book.

Name ....

Address ....

....

....

If you would prefer to pay by credit card, please complete:
Please debit my Visa/Access/Diner's Card/American Express (delete as applicable) card no:

Signature ....

Expiry Date ....